"NICK, WOULDN'T YOU LIKE TO TAKE ME up those stairs and ravish me, like Clark Gable ravished Scarlett in *Gone with the Wind*?" Dusty asked, her voice seductive.

"Take a look at those stairs, Dusty. I'm not even sure your hoops would make it up there. As for the ravishing"—he paused—"I thought we'd already decided that wasn't a good idea."

"Maybe we were wrong," she murmured.

A minor tremor raked his body at the thought of what she was suggesting. At the sudden strong urge he had to comply. He almost took a step toward the stairs, then turned her toward the parlor and into a shadowy corner.

"Dusty, you haven't been nipping at the brandy to get into the mood for your story-telling, have you?"

She flung her head back and smiled wickedly. "Don't tell me you don't want me . . ."

"If you don't stop that," he managed to say as her lips grazed his chin and nibbled on his earlobe, "the tour group's going to catch us behaving in a very naughty manner."

"Kiss me," Dusty said breathlessly. "Then I'll behave . . ."

WHAT ARE *LOVESWEPT* ROMANCES?

They are stories of true romance and touching emotion. We believe those two very important ingredients are constants in our highly sensual and very believable stories in the LOVESWEPT *line. Our goal is to give you, the reader, stories of consistently high quality that may sometimes make you laugh, sometimes make you cry, but are always fresh and creative and contain many delightful surprises within their pages.*

Most romance fans read an enormous number of books. Those they truly love, they keep. Others may be traded with friends and soon forgotten. We hope that each LOVESWEPT *romance will be a treasure—a "keeper."* *We will always try to publish*

LOVE STORIES YOU'LL NEVER FORGET
BY AUTHORS YOU'LL ALWAYS REMEMBER

The Editors

Loveswept ® 717

IMAGINARY LOVER

SANDRA CHASTAIN

BANTAM BOOKS
NEW YORK · TORONTO · LONDON · SYDNEY · AUCKLAND

IMAGINARY LOVER

A Bantam Book / November 1994

If you would be interested in receiving protective vinyl covers for
your Loveswept books, please write to this address for information:

Loveswept
Bantam Books
P.O. Box 985
Hicksville, NY 11802

ISBN 0-553-44443-3

Published simultaneously in the United States and Canada

Bantam Books are published by Bantam Books, a division of Bantam Dou-
bleday Dell Publishing Group, Inc. Its trademark, consisting of the words
"Bantam Books" and the portrayal of a rooster, is Registered in U.S.
Patent and Trademark Office and in other countries. Marca Registrada.
Bantam Books, 1540 Broadway, New York, New York 10036.

PRINTED IN THE UNITED STATES OF AMERICA

OPM   0 9 8 7 6 5 4 3 2 1

AUTHOR'S NOTE

My thanks to David Thomas, Betty Hirt, Michael C. Hidalgo, and the staff at the ART Station for allowing me to use them in this book. The ART Station's *A Tour of Southern Ghosts* is a remarkable fund-raising project for a worthy cause, and I salute those people who volunteer their support.

Also a special thanks to Nancy Knight, who gave me the idea for this book and is both my spell-checker and my guardian angel. In addition she can go anywhere and never get lost. If I ever take a ship to the stars, I want her to sail it.

ONE

Dusty O'Brian opened the door of the cab of the giant eighteen-wheeler, let her feet dangle in the air for a minute, then slid out and dropped to the ground.

"So long, Buddy," she said, "thanks for the ride."

Dusty started up the grassy embankment, then stopped to thread her arms into the straps of her backpack. The burly truck driver opened his window, leaned across the seat, and called out one last concerned warning, "Next time take a bus. Hitching a ride with an old friend is one thing, but there're some bad guys out there on the road. After what you've been through, I wouldn't want anything else to happen to you."

"Neither would I," Dusty agreed with a tired sigh. "But I'm as close as I'm gonna get to where I was headed."

Traffic on the Georgia freeway beside them barreled past, buffeting her with wind. She gave a wave to the driver as he eased his enormous vehicle back to the road and moved off into the October night.

A part of her wanted to climb right back up into the cab of that truck and keep on going, to see new places then leave them behind before they had time to make an impression on her.

A mirage, an illusion. That's what she wished she were, a veil of smoke, moving through the night, disappearing into the air unseen. If she weren't real, she couldn't hurt.

A car horn blasted and brought her back to the present, to the noise, the smell of exhaust fumes, and the hunger that roiled in the pit of her stomach.

With a sigh, she turned and climbed the hill. When she reached the city street she was looking for, she disregarded Buddy's advice and held out her thumb. According to her best recollection, the little village of Stone Mountain was off Memorial Drive a few miles up ahead.

Memorial Drive. Dusty wondered briefly what event this six-lane highway filled with fast-food restaurants and strip shopping malls was meant to memorialize. Indulging the appetite, she decided, and considered stopping for a burger. Then she remembered her empty pockets and kept moving.

At that moment an elderly woman stopped

her car and rolled down the window. "What's a pretty girl like you doing hitchhiking?" she asked in a worried voice. "You get in here quick."

Dusty dumped her backpack in the rear of the car and climbed in. The old woman reminded Dusty of Martha, one of the street people she had once kept a protective eye on, until the woman vanished one day. To Dusty, Martha was just another of the people she had cared about who had deserted her along the way.

"Where are you going, child?"

"Stone Mountain."

"It's pretty late to be sightseeing."

"The village, not the park," Dusty said, and wished she'd taken the city bus they'd fallen behind.

"Well, I can take you to the edge of town. I'm going to visit my daughter. She lives in one of those new apartment complexes along West Mountain Drive. I don't know why she can't find a young man and settle down, but no—she drives into Atlanta every day to study law. Wants to be a criminal lawyer, can you imagine that?"

A criminal lawyer was the last thing Dusty wanted to imagine. She'd seen enough of them, the charity-appointed kind who took your case, met you at the door to the courtroom, and asked for a quick rundown on the facts on the way inside. Dusty didn't answer.

Luckily, she didn't have to say a word. Her

Good Samaritan kept up a running conversation about the area, her family, and friends. Dusty had forgotten how old ladies could go on and on. She wondered if Aunt Hattie had turned into an old woman. Hattie was the only person Dusty had left in the world.

Though Hattie couldn't have loved Dusty more, she wasn't even Dusty's real aunt. Dusty was the child of a young actress Hattie had befriended, a woman who'd suffered through a long illness and later died. Hattie had taken in an orphan and given her a home.

There'd been a time when Dusty had listened for hours to her aunt's exciting tales about her career as a stage actress, a career that had dried up and left Hattie with no focus for her life's energy. Until she'd been offered a glorious role that would take her back to Broadway, then later on the road.

Reluctantly, she'd arranged to send Dusty to boarding school, but Dusty, rebellious and feeling like an old overcoat conveniently abandoned when a new style came along, gave in to a temper tantrum in the midst of an argument and ran away.

It hadn't taken Dusty three days to decide that she'd made a mistake. But she knew her aunt; if she went back, the good-hearted woman would never take the role she'd been offered. She'd already spent five years caring for Dusty; it wouldn't have been fair to Hattie.

So Dusty had kept going. As time passed, being away got easier.

Later she read in the newspaper that Hattie had been nominated for an award for her performance, and Dusty knew that she'd made the right choice. Eventually Dusty called Hattie, giving her glowing reports on how well she was doing on her own, but she never allowed herself a visit. She'd survived initially by living with a clan of homeless people in Florida. With the help of some counselors who'd taken a special interest in her, she eventually completed high school, two years of night school, and at last, the Florida State Police Academy.

But just when she thought she'd finally found her place in the sun, that place had been taken away, and Dusty came to believe that she was destined to be a vagabond. She'd hit the road, never admitting until she stepped off the truck that she was going home, back to Hattie.

Dusty was beginning to wonder if her driver knew where she was going, when the elderly woman turned off the busy highway and took a back street. "This is it," she said as she came to a stop at the corner. "I go straight."

"Thanks for the ride. Good night, and ma'am," Dusty cautioned, "it isn't a good idea for you to pick up hikers, even if they are women. I could have easily robbed and hurt you."

The elderly woman's eyes widened and she

gasped. Dusty closed the door and heard the click of the locks as the woman drove quickly away.

Dusty felt vaguely guilty for having frightened the woman who'd been kind to her, then faced the reality of her warning. There might have been a time when lonely old women could be kind to strangers, but no more. A woman couldn't even trust her own friends. Dusty was living proof of that.

Moments later Dusty was on the crowded, brightly lit sidewalk. There were shops, restaurants, small businesses, all quaint and inviting. She turned into a craft shop.

"Where is the ART Station?" Dusty asked a clerk behind the counter.

"Go half a block and turn to your left. It's the old railroad depot on the corner. Hey, I like your costume. Are you auditioning as a storyteller?"

Dusty shook her head and moved off again. Her costume? She brushed the dust from her jeans, then glanced into a shop window and gave up. She'd been traveling for three days, and she did look scruffy—dangerous even—wearing black and carrying all her worldly belongings on her back.

Dusty shrugged. What did she care what people thought?

Dusty came to the ART Station, gave it a passing glance, then turned down the street beside it, walking slowly, until she came to the two-

story white Victorian house on the corner beyond.

Four Twenty-Two. The script letters spelled
out the number over the door. The porch light
was on, but the door was locked, and nobody
answered the bell. Finally Dusty moved around
to the back door. It was locked as well. At least
there was a swing on the porch. Dusty threw her
backpack onto the swing, stretched out, and laid
her head on it. She'd been in worse places. Moments later she was asleep.

It was the smell of tobacco that woke her.
The sound of a board creaked in the darkness.

Someone was out there.

Correction. Someone was on the steps. As if
she'd never stopped using a finely trained instinct, Dusty considered the possibilities.

It wouldn't be Aunt Hattie. She wouldn't be
slinking into her own house. She'd use the front
door. At best, the intruder was some sort of
Peeping Tom; at worst, a burglar intent on theft.
Dusty knew that if she made the slightest movement, she could give herself away.

Whatever she did had to be quick, all in one
motion, a complete surprise. If she hadn't been
so tired, it might have occurred to her that a
burglar wouldn't be smoking. If she hadn't been
awakened from a sound sleep, she might have
realized that the man was sitting, not standing,
on the step.

If Nick Elliott hadn't been concentrating so

hard on trying to bring back the still-missing pieces of his memory, he'd have known he wasn't alone. When the swing creaked, he turned, straight into the force that caught him in the chest and catapulted him into the yard. Before he could react, someone rolled him onto his stomach and pulled his wrists together behind him.

"What in hell?" he said.

"Don't move! You're in big trouble, fella!"

It was a shocking realization to learn that the intruder sitting astride his waist was a woman, a strong woman with tight thigh muscles and hands of steel. "In trouble for what?"

"Attempted breaking and entering."

"The only thing breaking here is my back. And I can enter any time I like, you wildcat. I live here."

"You do?" Dusty let her captive go and slid to her knees beside the prostrate man. "I'm sorry, I thought this was Hattie Lanier's house."

"It is. Do you attack people at random, or do you do it by some special selection process?"

Dusty stood and moved away. She'd done it again, opened herself up to blame and ridicule. "Sorry," she said, "my mistake."

The man stood awkwardly. It was then she realized that he was crippled in some way. "Damn! I didn't mean to hurt you. Let me help." Not only had she tackled someone who apparently belonged there, but she'd body-slammed a handicapped man.

"You didn't have anything to do with it," he said with a growl, then turned and gave her such a glare of anger that she could see it in the dark. She could have been facing the devil himself. He was tall, thin, almost gaunt, with eyes that pierced right through her.

She recognized someone at the breaking point. She'd seen the same kind of reaction in a Vietnam vet fighting a flashback. Dusty backed slowly away, holding her hands up in a gesture of placation. "Okay, fella. Fine. Whatever you say. Can I call someone to help you?"

"I don't need any help!" he said. He pushed past her, stumbling over her backpack. "And if you've come for a handout, or you're another one of those crazy fans looking for some memento, you're too late. I've been told not to let anybody in until everything's been officially inventoried. And don't call me fella."

He fumbled for a moment with his key, then moved inside, slamming the door behind him. She heard the loud click in the darkness. The devil had locked her out.

"Son of a—" She kicked the bottom step and swore. She hadn't even asked about Hattie. With her hands on her hips she strode into the yard and looked up at the second floor. A light came on in the corner room, then switched off again. She knew he was standing there at the window, staring down at her. She was tempted to make an obscene gesture, then felt that familiar curtain of control slide back into place.

So, what to do? Hattie wasn't at home, and Dusty didn't think the man she'd tackled was ready to be friends.

Once again she was on the outside looking in. What was new about that? She caught sight of the cigarette he'd been smoking still smoldering in the dry October grass. Grinding it out with the heel of her boot, she stalked back to the porch and reclaimed her spot in the swing.

What did he mean about claiming a memento? Of course Hattie was famous, or she had been once. It was hard to believe that people would try to take something of hers after all this time. And who would be itemizing her belongings? Dusty was too tired to worry about that now. Handouts she could understand. Hattie had been famous for giving them.

Her aunt must be selling the house. Or maybe she was on the road again. He'd been left in charge and was taking his job seriously. At least he'd confirmed to Dusty that she was in the right place.

If there was a right place. It had been thirteen years, but this was still the house where she'd come once before when she'd needed a safe haven. In the morning she'd explain who she was and that she only wanted to stay until she could find a job, until she could find a place of her own where people didn't know her by name. If Hattie knew she were there, she wouldn't turn her away.

Dusty O'Brian didn't care much about starting over. She was better at leaving. Starting over promised a future; she didn't have one. The present was all she had. She might as well get used to it, beginning with spending the night in the swing.

Nick Elliott stood in the window and looked down at the silhouette of the woman in the yard below. He'd been totally surprised by her presence, though he shouldn't have been. There'd been a string of curiosity seekers. Hattie was famous for taking in strays, and Nick thought he'd seen most of them in the last few days. But somehow he didn't think this woman was a down-on-her-luck artist or actress.

This was a woman accustomed to being in charge. Everything about her said that, from her harsh voice to her firm body. She gave the impression that she belonged and he was the outsider.

There'd been a time when he would have been a better match for her, when he might have been the one to pin her down beneath him. A time before his body had been ravished by injury and the healing that stripped him of his dignity and his strength.

There was a time when he'd been the best

racquetball player at the club where he worked out. Now he was lucky to take a slow jog around the park without getting muscle spasms in his leg.

Gingerly he rubbed his kneecap, trying to still the throbbing. But it wasn't the injury or the healing that he was beginning to recognize; it was a need more fundamental than that— the need of a man's body for physical release— the reaction of that body to the presence and the touch of a woman.

"Damn!" She'd had him in a scissors hold and was ready to string him up as a burglar before he'd known what was happening.

Nick frowned. Surely Hattie would have warned him if she'd been expecting somebody special.

He assumed the woman was one of the many who'd suddenly appeared at the door after Hattie's death notice had run in the newspaper. They'd all wanted the same thing, just something to remember Hattie by. Some had even resorted to sneaking in and helping themselves.

The silhouette of the woman below gradually took on form and substance as the light from the moon etched her shape in the darkness. She was tall, her hair long, probably caught with a clasp at the neck. She stood, one arm folded across her chest, rubbing her other arm as she stared up at his window.

He could feel the challenge of her posture. But more, he could feel a kind of pain.

After a long moment she ground out the burning cigarette he'd dropped and disappeared out of sight onto the porch below. Whoever she was, she wasn't giving up. He'd probably find her in the swing come morning.

Nick shrugged his shoulders and rolled his head around, trying to stretch the still-present kinks that had come from sitting day after day in a hospital room. Waiting for someone to die was more exhausting than waiting for someone to get well. The body fought both.

"I've got to get out of here," Hattie had argued up to the end. "I've told stories on *A Tour of Southern Ghosts* since it started seven years ago. And I don't intend to miss this time, Nick Elliott. You just get these doctors on the ball and get me well!"

Nick had nodded and promised to use his influence to hurry the treatment. But he no longer had any influence, and after surgery that had been too late, all he could do was sit beside her and wait, listening to the drip of the fluid in the bag connected to her arm, like the ticks of a clock. He'd buried her three days ago.

Now he was bone tired, too tired to worry about some homeless woman who'd decided to take up residence on Hattie's porch. Hattie might have invited her in, but Nick had been told to keep out any intruders. He pacified his conscience by telling himself that even though it was October, it wasn't a cold night. She had a backpack and, from the shape of it, a sleeping bag as well. Hattie wouldn't want him to have her arrested. He'd just leave her alone.

Hattie's attorney would be at the house in the morning to talk about what was to be done with her things. He'd promised to carry out her wishes. Any other lawyer would handle the details from an office, but Hattie always made people come to her, and this would be her last command performance.

Stripping off his clothes, Nick turned on the shower and waited for the water to get hot. In the darkness he stepped inside and let the heat pepper his body. Showering in the dark was as much a defense mechanism as an economy. If there was no light, he couldn't see. But even the darkness didn't keep him from . feeling the sunken place at the site of the wound on his leg or the scar on the side of his face.

And the darkness didn't stop him from hearing Hattie's voice. "Nick Elliott, you might not be ready to play major league ball, but you're still a doctor. So you can't stand up and operate. Find a stool and sit down!"

But he couldn't even do that. When the hospital staff had invited him to assist in Hattie's case, he'd refused. "She's like family," had been his excuse. "Doctors don't treat their own family."

Nobody else had to know that he couldn't trust his memory. Nobody but his own physician knew how much medical knowledge he'd lost in the accident. "Selective amnesia," his friend and colleague had explained. "Your memory will likely come back, when you're ready to remember."

For now, he'd keep his secret. If Hattie's will called for her house to be sold, he'd buy it. The larger home overlooking the golf course, where he'd once lived, was still empty. He hadn't been back except to get his clothes and his secondhand car, the one Lois had refused to drive.

This Victorian house had become his hiding place, his security blanket, his haven from pain. The world didn't need to know that the surviving half of the most exciting couple in Atlanta, the most brilliant young surgeon in town, had quit practicing medicine.

Even if the accident hadn't stopped him, Hattie's death would have done it. He'd loved two women in his life. Both of them had died, and he hadn't been able to do a thing about either. One death he'd caused, and the other he couldn't stop.

With his hair still wet and his body thrumming with heat from the shower, Nick fell across the bed and pulled up the covers. Exhaustion swept over him, and moments later he was asleep. But the accident, the pain, and the woman from his past were blotted out of his mind by dreams of a shadow woman sleeping on the porch.

From her spot in the swing, Dusty had heard his footsteps moving back and forth. Then came the sound of water running through a pipe in the floor overhead. After a long time it hushed, and she heard him walk back. Then she heard a creak followed by silence.

Who was this intense man who slept in her aunt's house? And where was her aunt? Dusty hadn't necessarily expected to be welcomed with open arms, but she hadn't expected Hattie to be gone either. Granted, Hattie hadn't known she was coming. Hell, Hattie hadn't even known where Dusty had been for most of the last five years. Dusty had disappeared the first time because of misplaced anger, but that had been replaced by guilt, then shame, and finally necessity.

Dusty changed her position, then tried moving to the floor where she climbed into her bag. The temperature was growing cooler and the silence was beginning to close in on her. She'd spent too many nights in the kind of silence that echoed off the walls and pressed against her. Even the crickets had stopped chirping.

Finally she got up and sat on the step. "I live here," the man had said.

Dusty let out a long sigh. She wished she had a cigarette. She wished she hadn't given up smoking. But she'd been a police officer, and if there'd been anything in Dusty's life she'd wanted, it was to be a good officer, to be a good example for those she'd tried to help. And, dammit, she had been.

How could things have gone so wrong?

Dusty wished she could take a shower and find a real bed.

She wished she'd called Aunt Hattie and told her she was coming. Why was she sitting outside in the dark when she could be inside, sleeping on a soft bed? Part of being a good police officer was learning how the bad guys worked. And Dusty had been the best. She could get into the house if she wanted to, and suddenly she did. She needed to feel like she belonged.

A few minutes later, thanks to some training by one of her parolees, Louie the Rat, she was in the kitchen. Dusty stood still and listened. Instinct told her that there was nobody in the house but the unpleasant man upstairs and herself. It was too quiet.

That being the case, she'd just help herself to a snack before she found a soft place to sleep. The refrigerator was practically empty, which was not the way Dusty remembered it. Her aunt had always kept plenty of food on hand. There ought to have been all kinds of exotic leftovers carefully labeled and put away. Of course, she'd been a lot more impressionable the last time she'd looked, and so had her aunt.

Standing there, drinking straight from a carton of orange juice, she remembered how she'd felt when she first came to Aunt Hattie's—warm, grateful, and adequately fed. Hattie always had stories to go along with the picnics they'd had on the kitchen table. Dusty had been entranced by the woman who'd eaten Greek food on Malta and sushi in Japan.

Hattie had been a modern-day Auntie Mame to a young girl whose mother was dying. Afterward Hattie had pronounced that she'd never had a niece, and Dusty was forever assigned to play that role. That was a long time ago, before Dusty had run away and discovered the bad things in the world.

As a child Dusty had been told by her mother that there were two kinds of people, the haves and the have-nots. And you were assigned a number at birth. You might be allowed a little taste of the good life along the way, just enough to make you want it, but in the end, your die had already been cast.

Dusty emptied the juice carton and felt her way to the living room. The overstuffed couch was still where it had been all those years ago. Unfolding the ever-present afghan, she lay down and spread the crocheted throw over her. At least it was better than the ground.

In the morning she'd find Aunt Hattie and the man with the haunting dark eyes. Her last waking thought was that the man was right; he wasn't just any fella. If she had to give him a name, she'd call him Merlin.

TWO

"It's about time you got here."

Dusty heard the voice, yet it didn't seem quite real. It was more like a warm, comfortable dream. From some faraway smoky place a path had appeared, and she'd dashed forward toward a familiar warmth.

"Aunt Hattie?"

"Of course," the voice said with a chuckle. "Who else did you expect? Joan Crawford was busy and Ethel Merman has a terrible case of laryngitis. Serves her right for taking that last role from me. Of course, she can sing and I can't, but her acting was lousy."

Dusty sat up. She'd forgotten her aunt's ongoing feuds with other actresses. They'd been mostly a figment of Aunt Hattie's vivid imagination, but none of Hattie's friends had ever pinned her down about them.

"Aunt Hattie, who is that man upstairs?"

"Nicky? Nicky is a dear friend. He came to me the same way you did. He needed love and a place of refuge."

"Nicky?"

"Well, I am the only one who calls him Nicky."

"I can believe that. He isn't the most lovable man I've ever met."

"Oh, but he is, or he will be. Trust me, Dusty. Have I ever lied to you?"

Dusty held back a laugh, turning her face toward the voice coming from the corridor. "You? Lie? Of course not. But you do exaggerate now and then. Remember the wizard?" It was the voice of Dusty as a little girl that admonished with a pout, "You promised I'd meet him one day, Aunt Hattie. You said—"

Dusty broke off. There was no one there. Even in the soft darkness, Dusty could see that the corridor toward the kitchen was empty. "Aunt Hattie?"

There was no answer. Only the eerie sound of Dusty's voice echoed down the vacant hallway.

Still half-asleep, Dusty came to her feet and walked back to the kitchen. The door to the yard was closed. There was no sign of Hattie. Only a creak of the upstairs floor reminded Dusty that she wasn't alone.

Shaking her head, she headed back to the

couch. It must have been a dream. Sweet Jesus, she'd had enough of them through the years, but never quite so real. Pulling the afghan back over her, she closed her eyes and tried to go back to sleep.

But all she could remember was the wizard. He'd been a character Aunt Hattie had met on the Orient Express. She'd sworn that he'd stepped right out of a James Bond movie, mysterious and elegant. He'd been tall and thin, Aunt Hattie had said, with eyes that burned in their sockets.

Eyes filled with fury.

Like the man upstairs.

Dusty shuddered and pressed her eyes tighter. She tried to remember why she and Hattie had wanted the wizard to reappear, but the rest of the tale escaped her. Gradually Dusty felt the tension slip away as she fell asleep once more. It had been years since she'd thought of the wizard, though once he'd been her imaginary secret friend. She couldn't recall any more of the details of the story, only her name for Hattie's mysterious companion. As a child, she'd called the wizard Merlin.

A jarring sound brought Dusty awake again, this time into a crouching position on the balls of her feet. She automatically reached to her hip for her gun, only to remember that it wasn't there any longer.

"Hey, it's only the doorbell," a male voice said, "not a firing squad."

Dusty jerked around, trying to orient herself to the strange surroundings. Her gaze fell on the man coming down the steps.

He was whipcord thin, with great dark eyes and heavy brows. But it was the hypnotic effect of those eyes that she couldn't turn away from, the same mesmerizing effect that she'd felt when she'd been assigned to the unit protecting the magician David Copperfield at his Miami appearance.

The doorbell rang again.

Dusty forced herself to come back to a standing position as he descended the stairs. He was holding a mug in his hand. "I don't know how you got in here, but I guess I'm not surprised. There's coffee on the stove. Pick out whatever you're interested in, and if it isn't valuable, you can take it along when you go."

He walked past her as if finding a strange woman asleep on the couch was an everyday occurrence.

Dusty's "When I go?" was drowned out by the sound of the door opening. A man in a suit carrying a briefcase entered. An attorney, Dusty realized; she could smell one a mile away.

"Good morning, Nick," he said, giving Dusty a curious glance, then moving into the living room and taking a straight chair next to the couch. "Who is your guest?"

"Another curious fan. They've been coming out of the woodwork."

The attorney continued to stare at Dusty. "You look familiar."

"So do you," Dusty answered. She could have said she'd seen enough attorneys in the last year to recognize one from a hundred yards.

"Nick, I know that Hattie's request that I come here must seem a little strange to you," the attorney said. "I'm just following her wishes."

"I know. She told me to expect you. I'm just not sure why I'm involved."

"I'll get to that." He looked once more at Dusty. "This is confidential," he began. "What is your name, young woman?"

"Dusty O'Brian, and don't worry, I'm out of here."

The attorney came to his feet. A broad smile curled his lips. "Dusty. Of course! So you finally came back."

"Yeah, that mean something to you?"

"I just wish you could have made it sooner."

"Believe me, fella, if I could have made it sooner, I would have."

"I'm John Ralston Reynolds, Jr., your aunt's attorney. I suppose you have proper identification?"

"Don't worry, J.R., all the necessary information has already been forwarded to the local authorities. I'll be a good girl and follow orders. I won't make any trouble for Aunt Hattie."

Mr. Briefcase looked puzzled. "I beg your pardon?"

Dusty was listening to the attorney's strange conversation, but she couldn't get past the man sipping his coffee by the staircase. He was studying Dusty as if she were a frog about to be dissected. No, not a frog, a butterfly, pinned to a specimen board and unable to move.

"When will Aunt Hattie be back?" she asked, drawing her attention back to the attorney. "I ought to tell her why I'm here."

Ralston frowned and took a step toward Dusty. "You don't know?"

Merlin answered for her. "I haven't told her. I didn't know who she was. I thought when we met last night that she was either another one of Hattie's strays or a grief-stricken fan."

"Know what? Cut the crap! What's going on here, fella?"

This time she got a response from dark-eyes, a scowl that would clabber milk. "I told you last night, my name isn't fella. I'm Nick Elliott, and I buried Hattie Lanier three days ago."

Dusty's sharp retort died in her throat. It slammed down into the pit of her stomach and sucked out all the air, drawing into a spasm of pain she hadn't expected. It had been a long time since she'd hurt, since she'd let anything hurt her. She'd closed off the pain, but never the guilt.

This time the guilt came out of nowhere.

Hattie was gone, dead. The memory of this place and the woman who'd loved Dusty had been hidden behind tough street talk and the claim that Dusty O'Brian didn't need anybody. Aunt Hattie had always been here if and when Dusty ever needed her. That knowledge had carried her through the bleak times. Now Hattie was gone. Dusty was too late.

Dusty turned slowly around and walked back through the kitchen and out the door. She made her way to the big oak tree at the end of the yard and looked up. It was still there, the tree house that she and Hattie had built. Even the boards nailed into the tree that provided the steps. She climbed up and settled down with her head hunched over her knees, her eyes closed.

She was too late. Her past was completely gone now, along with any chance of a future.

"Who is she, Reynolds?"

"She's Hattie's niece. At least Hattie claimed she was. I don't know for certain that they're blood relatives, but Hattie took her in as a child and raised her."

"Raised her?"

"Well, until she ran off when she was fifteen. Hattie always felt responsible for that. She'd been offered a role on Broadway that would eventually put her on the road again. When Dusty found out that Hattie was sending her to boarding school, Dusty got the idea that she was being abandoned and ran off. But Hattie never gave up hope that she'd come back. From time to time there'd be a telephone call, but for the last two years, there was nothing."

"Odd," Nick said, "she never mentioned a niece to me."

"Until she got sick, I had the feeling that you two didn't do much talking."

Nick winced. Reynolds was right. As a patron of the ART Station he'd met semiregularly with the board and with Hattie. There'd been nothing special between them . . . before his accident. But the day he'd left the hospital, Hattie had been there to pick him up and bring him home with her. He hadn't cared where he went. He knew he didn't want to go back to the house he'd shared with Lois, so he'd agreed when Hattie had offered him a room. Another man would have been depressed, but Nick simply closed off what had happened and waited for his body to heal.

Hattie never reprimanded him, never intruded, never tried to force him. She was simply there, ever cheerful, ever confident that time would take care of everything.

When had he begun to relax and allow Hattie into his life? It had happened a little at a time, a request that he couldn't refuse, a special dish that she really needed him to taste. Then as time passed he began to notice that some of her requests weren't simply interfering. She couldn't do the things she'd always done, and it galled her to admit that she couldn't.

But why had she never mentioned this smart-mouthed, street-tough woman with the long legs and flaxen-colored hair? He wondered why he hadn't noticed her hair in the moonlight. Nick couldn't see her body beneath the jeans, biker vest, and shirt she was wearing, but if she were nude—his breath caught at the thought of those long bare legs—if she were nude, he'd bet his last nickel there'd be a tattoo.

And this creature was Hattie's niece? Somehow that didn't jibe with the stagestruck wannabees, the poets, and the costume designers that usually moved through Hattie's house.

Of course, those people probably thought the same thing about him. He didn't act. He didn't belong to the ART Station Guild, nor was he a painter. In fact, there wasn't a creative bone in his entire body, including those that were still healing.

Nobody in the village ever asked about his past. Nobody at the ART Station ever pried, and until Hattie collapsed in pain in the kitchen, nobody ever knew that Nick Elliott was a doctor.

Was! That was the operative word here.

"You're right," he finally said to Reynolds. "We didn't talk much. I guess it must seem strange to you, Hattie letting me stay here for all these months."

"Nothing Hattie Lanier did ever surprised me, Nick. Taking you in was probably one of the more normal things she did. At any rate, I didn't expect Dusty to be here, but that simplifies what I came to tell you—if she actually is Dusty."

Nick gave a dry laugh. "After knowing Hattie, I don't think there's much doubt. Why should we expect her niece to be a normal, ordinary person?"

"You're right. And she needs to hear what I'm about to say. Would you mind asking her to come in?"

Nick minded. He minded like hell, but the sooner she got back inside, the sooner the attorney would be finished and the sooner he could make his offer to buy Hattie's house and get rid of them both.

He pushed open the screen door and stepped onto the porch. Her backpack still lay on the floor by the swing. But there was no sign of Dusty. He'd stepped into the yard and started toward the gate when he felt her. Not her gaze, the connection was not that direct. It was more a silent awareness of anguish.

He stopped, turning one way, then the other until he found the tree and noticed the boards nailed to the trunk. For all the time he'd lived here, he'd paid little attention to the clumsy structure nailed among the branches.

He could see her through the bare limbs, her

head down, her knees drawn up to her chest. From where he stood, he could feel her pain.

Why had the knowledge of Hattie's death hit her so hard? According to the lawyer, she hadn't been home since she was a teenager. Hattie hadn't even heard from her for two years or more.

But she was grieving, and she was doing it silently and alone.

He could understand that.

"Excuse me, Dusty, is it?"

She didn't answer. Only the flinch of her shoulders told him that she had heard.

"Hattie's attorney wants you to come inside. He has some kind of information he wants to give us about Hattie."

"Can't imagine what he has to say to me," she said in a voice more dead than alive.

"Same here, but for Hattie's sake, I guess we ought to listen."

"I don't think so."

"Suit yourself."

She raised her head and watched as he walked slowly back to the house, holding himself almost too erect, his steps measured, belying the barely perceptible limp. The sun caught the side of his face, focusing on the scar that ran from his hairline down the left side of his face.

He wore scruffy running shoes, tan cotton trousers, and a red knit pullover shirt. As though he was aware of her scrutiny, he stopped when he reached the porch, looked back at the tree for a long minute, then picked up her backpack and went inside.

Something had happened to him, something that left him scarred and secretive. How had he known Hattie? Surely he wasn't one of those gigolos who wormed his way into the confidence of an older woman with the idea of taking what she had.

No, Hattie didn't have anything except the house. She'd always spent what she had or given it away. And she'd never seemed interested in men. Dusty couldn't see Hattie taking a lover. She gave away pieces of herself to everybody along the way.

Still, the part of Dusty that had once made her a good police officer now made her consider all the alternatives. Hattie had looked after Dusty; Dusty owed her a debt of gratitude. She'd listen to what the lawyer had to say, if for no other reason than to protect her aunt's interests.

Feeling old and very sad, Dusty climbed down from the tree where she'd once hidden to smoke cigarettes and drink a forbidden beer she had managed to snitch from the fridge. She brushed off her jeans and wiped the toes of her boots on the back of her pants as she went back inside.

She didn't know what Mr. Briefcase and Merlin were up to, but she knew that she was out of options. If this place was off-limits, she might have to live in that tree house.

Hell, she'd known the worst. She'd lived on the streets once; she could do it again.

But she didn't want to live on the streets. Dusty O'Brian had a great yearning for the upstairs bedroom with the pink ruffled curtains and the white bookshelves stuffed with books and bears. If they were still there.

Hattie wasn't still there.

Dusty had waited too long.

Dusty came to her feet, pushing the chair back from the dining room table with a screech.

"Whoa now, J.R., I think somebody is singing the wrong song here. I don't want half ownership in this house. I don't even know this man."

Mr. Reynolds laid down the papers he was reading from and looked at Dusty. "Miss O'Brian, you may certainly sign over your half of the house to Dr. Elliott, or you may sell it to whomever you wish. There is only one stipulation: you must donate some of your time to the ART Station to receive Hattie's money. That includes her storytelling part of the upcoming *A Tour of Southern Ghosts*. Either way, one-half of this house is yours; the other half belongs to Dr. Elliott. Hattie was quite definite on that point."

"I'll bet, with a little suggestion from the—

doctor, did you say? What kind of doctor are you, anyway, a tree surgeon? Besides, Hattie didn't have any money."

"Oh, but she did," the attorney corrected. "Hattie always invested her money wisely, and through the years she has accumulated quite a large sum of money. She left it all to you, Miss O'Brian."

This time when the doorbell rang, the dark-eyed man she called Merlin opened it to admit a young woman wearing leotards, an oversized shirt, and a baseball cap. She hugged Nick Elliott, brushed the tears from her eyes, and moved into the room, followed by a neatly dressed man wearing a sport coat.

"I can't believe it," the newcomer was saying. "Hattie has been such a big part of the ART Station for so long that I don't know how we'll get along without her."

"And the storytelling," her companion said. "She's always had the best spot, the one in the house. It won't be the same."

The young woman looked up, taking in the attorney with his papers spread across the dining room table and Dusty, who was standing in the doorway, eyeing the newcomers with total disbelief.

"Oh, I'm sorry. Are we interrupting?"

"Don't worry about it," Nick said. "Hattie's front door should have been a revolving one. This is Dusty O'Brian, Hattie's niece."

The woman immediately came forward, hugging a shocked Dusty. "This is David Thomas, artistic director of the ART Station. And I'm Betty Hirt, educational director."

"Hattie was our biggest supporter," David said quietly. "I didn't know that she had a niece. Please accept our condolences."

Betty frowned. "You know, I seem to remember there was someone she was looking for. Didn't she hire a private detective once?"

"She's been trying to locate Miss O'Brian for a number of years," the attorney agreed. "I hadn't heard that she'd been found."

"Neither had I," Nick Elliott concurred.

"Well, I think that's about it," Mr. Reynolds said, gathering his papers and replacing them in his briefcase. "I'll leave it to the two of you to work out the details. Miss O'Brian, you can discuss your commitment to the ART Station with Betty and David. I would like you to stop by my office to verify your identify, just as a formality, you understand."

Dusty, still stunned by the proceedings, watched the man leave. Nick Elliott followed, spoke briefly to him, then closed the door and leaned against it.

For a moment Dusty had the insane desire to laugh. They were like bookends, Merlin holding up one side of the room while she held up the other.

"If you're going to take Hattie's place at the

station, Miss O'Brian," David said, "you need to come to rehearsal as soon as you feel up to it. You'll need to learn your story."

This time Dusty did laugh. "Whoa now. What in God's heaven makes you think that I have any intention of filling Hattie's spot? I've been known to tell an occasional whopper, but I've never rehearsed it in advance."

"*A Tour of Southern Ghosts,*" David explained, "is one way we raise money for the ART Station. Every Halloween we tell ghost stories at the old Southern plantation."

"Well, you'll just have to carry on without me."

"Maybe you'd better think about that, Dusty. Your refusal to help out could be expensive, ma'am," Nick said in an excessively sweet voice that became more of a threat than a comment as he added, "if you intend to claim your inheritance."

"My inheritance? No way. I'm not telling any story, and I'm not claiming anything. I'm not looking for a lifetime commitment, just a place to stay for a few days, then I'm out of here."

"I don't doubt that. By the way, how are you traveling, by motorcycle or broomstick?"

The two ART Station employees sized up the impending confrontation and quickly made their exit, reminding Dusty at the last minute that rehearsal started at seven and they were ready to honor Hattie's request that Dusty take her place, if she would agree.

"I don't know why you have to be so confrontational," Nick said, refilling his coffee mug. "If you don't want to live here, I'll make arrangements to buy your half of the house, and you can leave."

Leave. That was exactly what Dusty wanted. But she couldn't. She was stuck here for at least six months. Her probation transfer depended on it. "Damn! I can't go."

"Why? I'm certainly not holding you. If you leave now, you'll be out of Dodge before sundown."

"It isn't that simple, Merlin. I can't leave. I have to stay, whether I want to or not."

Nick's eyes narrowed. He couldn't imagine this woman ever being forced to do anything she didn't want to do. "Now I'm Merlin? Where'd that come from?"

For a moment Dusty's expression softened. "It's just a fantasy game Aunt Hattie and I used to play. We wished for imaginary people. We always gave them names."

"This isn't a game, Miss O'Brian. As for your not being able to leave, is it the money? I'll have Reynolds send you whatever you have coming."

"Fine, you do that. I'll be in the bedroom upstairs, the one with the pink curtains—if they're still there."

"They are. But I don't understand. You can

still collect Hattie's money, even if you live somewhere else."

"No, I have to stay here," she said, leveling him with a fierce gaze. "The Florida State Bureau of Pardons and Parole has ruled that I must. If I don't, I'll have to go back to Florida, and I don't ever intend to set foot in the state again."

It was Nick's turn to be confused. "What does the Florida State Bureau of Pardons and Parole have to do with your staying here?"

She looked at him, jutted out her chin, and answered. "Everything. I'm a police officer gone bad."

"I don't understand."

"What's not to understand, doctor? You'd better sleep light. Maybe even invest in a guard dog."

"After what happened last night, I believe that. What I'm still waiting to hear is why."

"Simple, Merlin. Your new roommate is an ex-con."

THREE

"Are you really Hattie's niece?"

The resonant quality of his voice intrigued Dusty. It bonded into a physical connection forcing her to turn to face him, when what she wanted to do was follow the attorney into the street and demand that he take back Hattie's bequest.

No, she decided, not Hattie's bequest, her absurd expectation. Dusty was still having trouble understanding her aunt's logic. How could the woman possibly have known that Dusty would ever return? How could she have accumulated the wealth that old J.R. had dangled before Dusty?

As for Dusty taking Hattie's place as the guardian angel for the ART Station, that was the most impossible expectation of all.

She realized the man standing quietly by the

stairs was silently demanding her attention with the strength of a laser beam reaching out and probing her mind. The beam was invincible, compelling, forcing her to acknowledge his question.

Dusty finally gave in to the demands of the dark-eyed man, and turned to face him. "No, as a matter of fact, I'm not Hattie's niece. I'm not related at all. Are you really a doctor?"

"Yes, or I was, a surgeon." There was no outrage, no questions, simply the statement of a fact. The slow, even cadence of his speech was meant to suggest nonchalance, though she sensed reluctant curiosity beneath the outer shell.

"And what are you doing here, making an extended house call?"

"No. I don't practice anymore. And I don't make house calls, so even though we're sharing the same quarters, don't ask."

Before Dusty could stop herself, she responded with the old "Touch me and die, fella" look that had always protected her.

Except this time it wasn't working. The man didn't back off. His injuries were physical; otherwise, he was as strong as she. And he was letting her know that without words.

"So, Merlin, I'm an intruder. What are you really, Hattie's flunky, or some con man who managed to wiggle into a lonely old woman's life?"

His mouth tightened slightly, signaling the anger that had transformed his already dark eyes into the inky blackness of a midnight storm.

"Hattie was neither lonely nor in need of a flunky," Nick answered. "She was a woman who gave far more than any person ever asked of her —and demanded little in return. She'd never expect more of you than you could deliver."

Dusty gave him a disbelieving look. "I don't call telling ghost stories a little demand."

"And I don't call it a big request in return for a fortune," he said.

"How did Hattie die, was she sick?" Dusty asked.

"Cancer. Don't worry, there are no other restrictions on you. I'm not sure that either of us is worthy of Hattie's gifts. But at least I was here for her. Where were you?"

"In jail," she snapped, "but you're right. I have no excuse for my behavior. I probably wouldn't have been here if I'd been free."

Why she was in jail should have been his question, but it was up to her to provide that information. Instead, he asked the thing that really held his attention. "Why'd you leave in the first place?"

"I was a hot-tempered little hellion who blew her chance with Hattie when I was fifteen. Since then I've had plenty of time to redeem myself and I didn't. So think what you like, Merlin, I don't give a—"

He continued to stare at her as if he were looking past her glib retort and absorbing the pain of her confession.

"Yes you do," he said, coming toward her, "and it's eating you alive. I know about guilt and pain and what it will do to you, and I can recognize it when I see it."

His index finger traced the curve of her cheek, rimming her lips and stopping at the indentation in her neck where her pulse was shimmying like an out-of-control hula dancer.

For a long moment they stood facing each other, sharing the heated breath of two equals, each determined to weaken the other's control. Her breath was coming in small pants, barely enough to expand her chest cavity. Only inches away his lips curled into a scowl. She thought he was going to swear.

He didn't.

He simply let go and stepped back. "Why do you keep calling me Merlin?"

"Hattie's Merlin was a man of mystery like you," she answered. "I never knew whether he was real or not. I always thought that he was one of Hattie's creations."

"Creations?"

"Isn't that what we both are? Figments of Hattie's imagination?"

He dropped his gaze and considered her absurd question. "You're right. I suppose both of us could have come from the dark side of Hattie's world, the demons she tried to tame."

"Merlin was no demon," Dusty corrected. "Merlin was a wizard. Hattie loved the idea of the mystery of his age-old wisdom and powers."

Dusty wasn't prepared for the quick smile on Nick's face, but she wasn't surprised at the speed with which it disappeared.

"A wizard? That's how you see me?"

She didn't answer his question directly. "So, you're not a wizard. If you're really a doctor, why are you hiding up there in Hattie's attic?"

"I told you, I don't practice medicine anymore."

"Does that have something to do with your limp and the scar on your face?"

"I don't limp!"

"And I'm Mary Poppins."

"Touché! Let's get you settled in your room." Nick picked up Dusty's backpack and started up the stairs. "I have to go over to the plantation house and check some loose bricks on the tour route. My car's at the station. Do you want to come along?"

"Not in—" She swallowed her remark. The good doctor looked as if he were making an effort at holding up a white flag by issuing a genuine invitation. If they were going to have to share the house, at least temporarily, it behooved her to find a way to do it with the least amount of conflict.

"I can't," she finally said. "I have to check in with the police chief. Part of my parole."

"The police station is nearby. I'll come along."

"You're sure you're not worried about being seen with an ex-con?"

He gave a dry laugh. "Not if you aren't worried about being seen with a murderer."

After they picked up Nick's car at the ART Station, they stopped by the office of the Chief of Police and found that he'd been notified of Dusty's pending arrival. Arrangements were made for her to report to a probation officer in the county, and she was promised that the situation would be kept confidential.

"Fat chance!" Dusty said as they drove away from the police department. "By nightfall every law enforcement officer in the county will know about the officer gone bad."

"So you'll be famous. My guess is that the news that you're Hattie's heir will be bigger."

Dusty caught glimpses of the huge stone mountain for which the city was named. It was gray and cold looking, imposing its presence on the landscape like a solemn judge. She gave a little shiver, remembering the first time she'd seen it, the time Hattie had brought Dusty and her mother home.

"Why'd she do it, Merlin?"

"I don't know. I don't even know why she took me in. That was Hattie. She just burrowed past the surface and found the pain. It was her way of feeding her own energy, finding a need for her help."

"Hattie was like a magnet, seeking the lost ones and bringing them back to life. Except for my mother."

"What happened to her?"

"Drugs, alcohol, hepatitis. Any one, or all three. Who knew? What's your claim to pain, Doc?"

"I caused a wreck in which my wife was killed."

"So, were you drunk or something? Why the guilt?"

Nick's hands tightened on the steering wheel. He'd never answered that question for Hattie; he couldn't imagine why he was formulating the words for this tough-looking woman.

"No, not drunk, just overcome with a stubborn, unreasonable ambition."

"I never arrested a driver for ambition."

"I'd worked twenty-four hours straight in Emergency. My wife was a nurse. She knew I was too tired to keep going. She urged me to let someone else take over. But I was Superman in scrubs. I was becoming more famous by the day. I was immortal. My patient died."

"So, no doctor can save them all," Dusty said softly.

"I thought I could."

"And what happened?"

Nick hesitated, then went on. "She wanted to drive, but I refused. I was full of anger and flying high on adrenaline. It was raining. I was driving too fast. You know the rest. She died, and I was in a coma for months. When I finally came out of it, I learned that she'd been expecting our child. I wanted to die. Hattie knew it, and she wouldn't let me."

"So, why don't you get back to work? You look okay now."

"I'm not!" he snapped, then let out a deep breath. "I'm just not ready to go back yet. Besides, Hattie needed me, and it was the least I could do."

They turned into the park and were waved past the guard's station when he saw the sticker through the car window. Nick drove along the wooded road, past beds of late-blooming flowers and joggers running along the wide sidewalks. Among the green pine trees, the leaves on the hardwoods were turning, dropping splashes of red and orange to the ground in a patchwork quilt of color.

"The first time I ever came here," Dusty said, "we rode a train that ran around the mountain. There were passengers dressed in costumes; girls in hoop skirts and men in frock coats. At one point Indians attacked the train, running down the aisle and kidnapping one of the women. It scared the pants off me."

Nick grimaced. Seeing this woman's legs without pants was becoming too constant a thought. She pulled the cap she'd been wearing from her head, allowing long straight blond hair to fall free across her shoulders. There was something symbolic about that gesture, as if she were freeing herself as a woman when she let her hair loose.

The fall breeze caught its strands and whipped them behind her, revealing a flush of color on a face that was too lean and too exposed.

"The Indian attack doesn't take place anymore. Probably politically incorrect. I guess the plantation wasn't here when you came."

"I don't know. If it was, we didn't see it."

"Well, it begins here, behind this fence. You can see the new Cobb house on the left. They're restoring it as they get the funds, but it's suffered a lot of damage from leaks since they moved it here."

Nick pulled into the parking area next to the entrance and stopped. At the gate, Dusty could see a number of smaller houses scattered across a green lawn like the pieces on a Monopoly board. Inside the gate was a long sidewalk, which they followed to the plantation house itself.

"This is it. The house dates back to 1850.

They found it on a thousand-acre plantation in south Georgia."

Dusty took a look at the graceful buff-colored antebellum plantation manor house with the green shutters and shook her head in disbelief. "How'd they get it here?"

"Betty Hirt said they had to cut it apart and bring it in on trucks."

"I expected it to be white, like Tara. How come it isn't, Merlin?"

"The story goes that a slave dropped his brush in the Georgia clay and turned the bucket of paint yellow. The lady of the house liked it and told him to keep "muddying it up."

"And all these other buildings?" she asked.

"For years the committee that planned the plantation gathered up buildings from everywhere, trying to reproduce an authentic successful Southern plantation, the kind people would expect to see."

Dusty glanced at the weathered outbuildings set away from the house—the barn, the elegant carriage house, and the smaller structure called the Overseer's House. "Was this typical?"

Nick laughed. "I don't think so. Actually, according to Hattie, this kind of aristocracy was mostly a myth, but there were some wealthy landholders who were able to create incredibly luxurious lifestyles. Hattie loved all this. She always thought she'd have made a grand lady of the manor."

Dusty was surprised at the enthusiasm in Nick's voice. She thought that Nick might have felt at home here as well. He might not believe that he was involved in Hattie's project personally, but his interest was obvious. "For a volunteer, you seem to know a lot about the place."

"I suppose I do. There's something about the plantation that gets to me. It's like an out-of-place relic, living on in a time where it doesn't belong." He hesitated, allowing himself for a moment to glance at Dusty, trying to judge her reaction.

"Yeah, I can see that. And all these people come out here prying, poking into its history and secrets as if they have a right to know. I don't know why the house doesn't swallow them up. Are there ghosts?"

"The two weeks before Halloween there are. As for the rest of the time, I don't know. There are stories, of course. But nobody talks much about them."

There was something odd in Nick's voice. He'd seen the ghosts or something. Dusty didn't know how she knew, but she did. The good doctor had made a psychic connection here somewhere, and Dusty found herself glancing around uncomfortably.

"I don't believe in ghosts," she said defiantly. "They're just bad dreams, nothing more. The dead don't really come back to haunt you. They sure can't give you orders."

"Hmm" was his only comment. "I have to meet David and Betty at the house. Do you want to come, or would you rather wander around?"

Suddenly Dusty didn't want to be alone. "I'll come with you. Might as well see Hattie's spot. You did say she had the choice location for telling stories."

"Yes, she did. She was the only one allowed in the house."

"What makes that the choice spot?"

"If the weather decides to turn nasty, you'll see. The other storytellers stand under trees, inside open barns, gazebos, and on the porches of other buildings. The house is warm and dry."

"What do you mean, I'll see? I am not telling a ghost story."

Nick stopped and turned to face her. "I had no intention of becoming involved in this either, but I am. And I think you will do what Hattie wanted. I think Hattie will see that you do, one way or another."

"She's already offered me a fortune, what else can she do? She's dead."

"True. But if you believe in ghosts—and Hattie did—she could reappear, couldn't she? This is her time of year, and this place is exactly the kind of dramatic setting Hattie would choose to make her presence known."

There was too much truth in Nick's statement. Dusty didn't want to think about that, especially after her disturbing dream. She searched for a way to change the subject and couldn't.

"Aunt Hattie a ghost?" Dusty remembered the dream she had, when Hattie had spoken to her. "You don't believe that, do you?"

"There are too many things that we can't explain, Dusty. I don't even try anymore. I just let life happen. In your street jargon you'd call it going with the flow."

"That translates to 'take the easy way out.' I can understand that, I guess."

"And with Hattie's money . . ."

". . . the way would be much easier," she finished his sentence, admonishing herself for even considering the idea.

"I thought you might see it that way," he said, and started up the walk to the house. They climbed the horseshoe stairs that led to the main floor.

"Nick, can you look right here?" Betty Hirt's voice called out from the roped-off drawing room at the end of the large foyer.

She was standing beneath the fireplace, studying the portrait over the mantle. "Does this portrait look different to you?"

Nick moved forward and looked up. He'd seen the portrait every day for the last month, but he'd never paid that much attention. The woman in the painting was a nameless figure, dressed in clothing of the mid-1800s. He'd remembered her hair as being an undistinguished shade of brown, covered by a net of some sort. Her eyes had been open wide, as if she were startled. On the shoulder of her faded cream-colored dress, she'd pinned a broach of pearls and gold filigree. The portrait was nothing particularly outstanding, just a good accent piece for Hattie to stand beneath while she told her story about the Confederate widow who'd waited in this house for her husband to return.

But today a quiver ran down Nick's back, exploding into a sharp pain in the hip area where he'd suffered the injury. There was something different about the painting. It seemed clearer. The woman's hair was lighter, the expression in her eyes more startled.

"Maybe," he admitted. "Maybe it's the light. I noticed earlier that the floor in front was showing wear."

David Thomas, standing behind Betty, stepped forward and studied the floor. "You're right. Perhaps we should consider moving the storyteller, maybe to the first rung of the stairs. Could we have Michael rig up some kind of hazy light that would give Dusty a ghostly effect?"

"Now, wait a minute," Dusty said. "I haven't said I was going to do it."

"Michael is wonderful at special effects," Betty agreed, "but Dusty would be in the way of the tour if we put her out here in the entrance hall."

Suddenly the portrait took a dive, the corner

of the frame hitting the mantle and falling neatly into Nick's hands. As he caught it, he brought the back of it to his chest, aiming the figure directly toward Dusty.

"Goodness," Betty exclaimed. "It's a good thing you were standing there, Nick." She let her gaze play back and forth between the painting and Dusty, who was staring at it in shock.

It was then that they all came to the same conclusion. The woman in the painting looked like Dusty, or like Dusty might have looked in 1864.

"Oh, no!" Dusty said sharply. "You aren't playing games with me. Even ghosts can't change paintings. I'll wait for you in the car, Merlin."

Before anyone could question her strange reaction, Dusty was striding down the walk toward the gate, her long legs making quick work of the distance. As she walked, Nick could almost see her wearing the rope net in the portrait. The hoop was a little harder to imagine, but when he visualized her bare legs beneath it, the picture fell into place.

He shook his head. It had been a while since his mind had gone squirrelly on him. Not since he'd left the hospital. At least not about routine things. It was his medical knowledge that continued to elude his memory. Sitting by Hattie's bed, trying to reconstruct what he knew about her condition and treatment, he had drawn a blank. But this was different.

Dusty O'Brian was bringing life to parts of his mind that he had never thought would function again.

That he'd never wanted to function again.

David brought a stepladder, and they rehung the portrait, stood back, and studied it again. Back in her place on the wall once more, the woman didn't look quite so much like Dusty. In fact, Nick wondered why she had disturbed them so much. From where he was standing, there was little about the two figures that seemed alike.

As for Dusty's strange outburst, he had no explanation. When he'd suggested ghosts and Hattie's return, he'd done it tongue in cheek. Though Hattie had often told him that she'd see him soon, he'd passed it off to her sickness—and her quirky sense of humor.

Still, he couldn't pass off the odd sensation of her presence he'd felt in the night. It was her home, and he didn't doubt that she'd imprinted herself on the very foundation of the house, but more than that he wasn't willing to concede.

Even more unexplainable was the unexpected arrival of Dusty O'Brian, as if Hattie had summoned her. If he'd tried to picture an adopted niece for Hattie, it would never be a woman like Dusty. There was an exuberance for life, a genuine caring inside Hattie that spilled over everyone and everything she touched.

But Dusty? She was dark and angry. A self-admitted failure. An ex-con, for Pete's sake. A person nobody would have given the time of day, except for Hattie.

A person much like himself.

Hattie's three protégés replaced the plex-iglass that kept visitors from entering the rooms, and left the house.

"Do you think she's going to do it?" David asked.

"You mean will Dusty take Hattie's place?" Nick asked. "I don't know."

Betty gave a discouraging groan. "If she doesn't, we're going to have to find a replacement quick. We're scheduled for the final rehearsal at the theater tonight. Starting Monday, we'll work at the stations on the grounds."

"I guess you'll find out tonight," David said. "She knows about rehearsal. All we can do is see if she turns up."

Their discussion turned more technical: ways to display the items they would sell, where to put the refreshment tent and Betty's powerful new two-way radio she hadn't yet learned to coordinate with those carried by the stage managers.

Nick left them at the gate and headed back to the car. Dusty was leaning back against the seat, her eyes closed. For all practical purposes she seemed to be sleeping. She didn't move until he started the engine and began to drive away.

"Are you sure you aren't a wizard?" she asked.

"I assure you, I'm not a wizard."

"Then how else do you account for what happened back there?" Her voice was light but troubled, and she couldn't conceal the tremor of her lower lip.

"Vivid imaginations working overtime. It's not unusual. People dealing with supernatural elements have already had to suspend a certain amount of disbelief. Therefore, they are often easily open to suggestion. We all saw something that wasn't there. Lord, I've done enough of that lately."

"You mean the woman in the picture didn't look like me? It just happened to fall off the wall and into the light so that we could see the resemblance?"

"Exactly. Now, I'm hungry. Let's get some lunch."

"Sorry, Merlin. Can't afford it. I'm tapped out."

"Don't worry. I'm buying."

"Are you rich, or did Hattie already settle half of her money on you?"

He narrowed his brows, hurt that she would even consider that he would accept Hattie's money. Then he remembered that he was not only willing to take half of the house, but wanted to buy the rest of it.

"The answer is really none of your business,

but I'll tell you. Yes, I'm rich, or I'm comfortably well-off. But it's money I made, not Hattie's."

"Why would you ask me to lunch?"

"Hell if I know. Why would anybody want to be seen with a woman who looks as if she's been on the trail for weeks, a trail that didn't pass by a hotel or a watering hole?"

Dusty looked down at her clothes and winced. He was right. She was a mess. Until now she hadn't cared. But as he pulled into the parking area beside a neat little white frame house sporting a sign that said Village Inn, she grimaced.

With Hattie gone she would be in grave straits, at least for a time. She'd have to find a job quick. Until then, she would make use of Hattie's washing machine. For now, if Merlin wanted to stake her to a meal, she'd take it. She did look like an escapee from a wagon train, but it was his choice to be seen with her.

It wasn't Dusty the patrons stared at as the waitress seated them, it was Nick. With his hand resting at the small of her back, the doctor guided her adroitly among the lunch-goers to a small table near the window. Gazes quickly slid past Dusty and settled on Nick.

Even without the flowing robes of a magician, there was a commanding stature about him that drew attention. If he were a rock star, he would never be able to disguise himself and walk freely among the masses; the force of his personality announced his presence.

The very touch of his hand on her body set off a shimmer of awareness that told Dusty how the women watching felt. The electricity was intensified to a disturbing proportion. She wanted to shimmy away, remove herself from his physical connection, yet she seemed caught up in some kind of force field that melded them together.

"Whoa!" she said, under her breath. "This is getting heavy. Cool it, Desirée."

Nick leaned forward, catching only the last of her words. "Desirée? The desired one. Is that your name?"

"Hell no, I'm Dusty. Desirée was a foolish twit nobody wanted."

Maybe, he thought to himself, and maybe she was so busy being a rebellious twit that she never knew. Gallantly, he assisted her to her chair and sat across from her. "Tie up your horse, Dusty, and let's eat."

FOUR

It had been a long time since Nick had invited a woman to lunch, and he was reasonably certain that it had been even longer since Dusty had been invited.

Later he couldn't remember what they ate, only that the meal had been pleasant, almost as if they'd decided to put aside everything that had happened and simply enjoy the food like two ordinary people—before the incident.

They talked about inconsequential things. She liked police action and mysteries on television, he liked science fiction and sports. She surprised him with the range of her reading, until she explained that she had read everything in the prison library, from history to the classics.

Then the woman at the table nearest them suddenly stood and began to gasp. Frantically she tried to clear her throat, beating her fists on the table in acute distress.

Dusty had taken first-aid classes during her time on the police force. Still, it took her a moment to recognize the problem. "Quick, Merlin, help her, she's choking."

Nick had moved to the woman's side and was glaring at her helplessly. He knew that Dusty was expecting him to do something. It wasn't that he was frozen, or that he had turned into some kind of limp noodle, rather the opposite was true. He was a writhing mass of coiled energy, ready to comply. He just couldn't remember what the hell to do. It seemed as if the moment stretched into forever, though he knew that everything was happening instantly.

"Nicky," Hattie's familiar voice cut in sharply. "Administer the Heimlich maneuver before she croaks. Don't worry. I've brought help, just put down your guard and let Siggy slip through."

In the blink of an eyelash a strangely garbed man with a beard was standing beside Nick clutching his rib cage in an exaggerated motion. Nick followed suit.

"You can do it, Doctor Elliott," the stranger said. "Arms around her and clamp down. Squeeze hard and fast. Then release her."

At first Nick's actions felt strange, then as he repeated them, his uncertainty fell away and suddenly he was acting on his own. Seconds later a piece of meat came flying out of the woman's mouth, and she gasped for air.

"You did it," Dusty said, giving him a hug.

Without thinking, Nick clasped Dusty's shoulders and pulled her close. He had done it. He could feel his heart pounding, the tension coiled there, and yet he felt a strength rushing through him, a wild exhilaration.

For a moment he simply held Dusty, and, too surprised to protest, she let him. Then, with a look of alarm at her reaction to his touch, she pulled away and watched as he calmly sat back down in his chair.

Her voice was uncharacteristically shaky as she said, "A little slow on the uptake, but you saved her, Merlin."

The rare show of emotion died. "No, it wasn't me."

"Well, I don't know who else you think it was. I was here, remember?"

It was hard to admit the cold, hard truth, but he refused to take full credit. "I couldn't have done it if that man hadn't told me what to do."

"What man? There was nobody here but you, me, and the waitress, Merlin."

Nick looked around. The woman was being escorted toward the ladies' room, and the rest of the diners were staring at him curiously. Nowhere was there a bearded man in a dark suit.

Thoroughly shaken, Nick hurried through the rest of the meal, paid the bill, and drove silently back to the house. He was having difficulty accepting what had happened, and he refused to give voice to his dilemma. The woman had been choking. But he hadn't had any idea what to do until he'd been directed.

And he was a doctor.

"You'd think she'd have at least said thank you," Dusty finally said as they went back in the house. "I mean how many times do you get a chance to thank a person for saving your life?"

Saving her life? The very thought made Nick tense. When he realized that Dusty was staring at him, waiting for some kind of response, he muttered, "It was nothing."

"Well, I thank you, even if she didn't. And I thank you for lunch as well. As soon as I can find a job, I'll treat you."

"Once you get Hattie's money," he said roughly, "you can buy the restaurant."

"I've told you before, I'm not taking Hattie's money."

"And I told you there was someone there, in that restaurant. A man with whiskers, wearing an odd-looking coat. And . . ." he faltered, "for a moment I thought I heard Hattie's voice."

"You're seeing things, Merlin. Better lie down for a while." But their banter had lost its bite. She was seeing the man as a doctor and remembering what he must have been to Hattie, how Hattie must have relied on him. Yet he took no credit for what he'd done, choosing instead to say someone else was responsible.

What was the man's problem?

Nick read the changing expression on Dusty's face. She was right. He had no intention of explaining; he still wasn't ready to admit to his memory loss. Maybe he'd take advantage of the out she was offering.

He'd take her advice to lie down before he made himself look like an utter fool, if he could get up the stairs without tripping. His limp was always more pronounced when he was tired or angry. Now he had to force himself to put weight on that hip, to keep from giving in to the pain as he climbed.

Nick Elliott was just tired. After months in a coma and even longer in physical therapy, he'd turned his back on the medical community and checked himself out of the hospital. Nick knew about mental abnormalities, not from a medical standpoint, but a personal one. He'd experienced what he'd been told were self-induced flashbacks of recrimination meant to punish himself for the accident. But this was different. He'd seen someone. And he'd heard Hattie speaking to him, as if she were standing right there in the restaurant.

"No, I'm not even going to consider that." He swore and pulled a cigarette from his pocket. Odd, he'd never smoked before the accident, when his life had slipped out of control. Now it was his way of spitting in the wind. He lit the cigarette and took a long drag.

The acid smoke filled his lungs. He let it out, slowly and deliberately, pacing his exhaling like the muttering of a mantra. But this time it didn't work. He didn't relax. The tension just lay there in the bottom of his stomach without release.

Suddenly he felt a presence. He looked around, expecting to see Dusty. She wasn't there.

"Just hold on to your shorts, Nicky. He was there, Dr. Freud. I know he's a bit out of date, but the good thing is he's managed to keep up with the old and learn all the new stuff as well. I told the old darling about your memory problem, and he came back to help."

Nick stubbed out the cigarette and swore. He'd been confused after the wreck. But once he'd realized what had happened, he'd made himself accept both his physical condition and, later, his memory loss. Never had he deluded himself.

Even during the worst of the horror he was forced to live with, he'd never hallucinated, never seen something or someone who wasn't there. And he wasn't going to start now.

"No," he said stonily. "Hattie's dead. I buried her. She isn't speaking to me. This isn't happening."

"Sure it is, Nicky. And it's all going to work out. Just like you told Dusty, just . . ." the voice wavered for a moment, growing dimmer as if it were moving away, ". . . go with the flow and look after her for me. You need each other."

Then Nick was alone, a fine film of perspiration dotting his forehead, his hands clenched in tight fists. He lay down and closed his eyes. As he lay, his hands uncurled and his body relaxed. The blanket that covered him moved so softly that he didn't wake. The aura of warmth gently settled over him.

There was a satisfied, musical laugh. "Poor boy, always fighting me. He'll learn."

By late afternoon Dusty had made her room livable and explored the rest of the house. She discovered an entire room filled with costumes and props. The costumes were a godsend because the only clothing she owned was the outfit she was wearing and one spare. In Hattie's wardrobe room she found an eclectic collection of skirts, jackets, and shawls she could wear.

And she found the scrapbooks.

There was book after book of photographs of Dusty growing up, beginning with her arrival as a thin, angry little ten-year-old and ending with a defiant frizzy-haired girl with too much eye shadow and a smart mouth. Hattie had chronicled every event. Lord knew how much Dusty had hated that, but Hattie had been in her element.

There was a program from her school play,

and ticket stubs from the numerous times Hattie had taken her to the theater. Dusty smiled grimly as she came across a playbill from a touring company's production of *Ghosts* autographed to her by the actress.

But it was the stack of letters beneath the scrapbooks that stopped Dusty in her tracks: letters from Hattie's agent. For the thirteen years since she'd run away, Dusty had thought that Hattie had grabbed at the chance to get rid of her and get back on the stage. She'd been wrong. There were many overtures from the theatrical world and all had been rejected with the excuse that Dusty needed her.

Hattie had put her life on hold until that last offer had come, the one she couldn't turn down, her last chance at Broadway. Dusty felt her throat tighten. It wasn't as if she hadn't known the truth, deep inside. She had. She had just been afraid that Hattie didn't want her anymore. And before Dusty could be rejected, she'd left.

All that time, Hattie had cared for Dusty, at her own expense. Now that it was too late, Dusty knew the truth. But the truth came with a price: following Hattie's last request. Dusty knew that she had to do what she could to make it up to the woman she'd hurt so badly.

Dusty would tell the damn story.

As clearly as if Hattie were standing there, Dusty heard her say, "Thank you, child, I knew you would."

Dusty showered, washed and dried her hair, then donned one of the gypsy skirts and peasant blouses that went well with her boots. Helping herself to Hattie's cosmetics, she fixed her face and pinned her hair back on one side with a rose. With a shawl of matching colors, she decided that she'd do her aunt proud, or as proud as a woman like Dusty could ever do.

As she started down the stairs she ran into the good doctor, who looked up at her and visibly started.

"You—you look very nice," he said. "Are you going out?"

"You know damn well where I'm going, you and Aunt Hattie and all the other spirits pulling the strings around here."

She didn't mean to sound so sharp. But as surprised as he was at her appearance, she was that much so at his. He'd changed into a bulky red turtleneck sweater and a pair of dark flannel trousers. Draped over one shoulder was a leather bombardier jacket with an insignia on the arm.

"What spirits?" he asked cautiously.

"The ones who hover around us, poking us in the direction they want us to go." She realized how she must sound and corrected herself. "Aw, forget it. I'm just on edge. I've never been a storyteller in my life. All this is giving me nightmares, and my knees are tap-dancing against my petticoat."

Nick allowed an amused grin to curl his lips for a second. "You'll do Hattie proud," he said. "Shall we go?"

"You're going to rehearsal too?"

"Yep, it's Hattie's night to be the station volunteer on call. I'm filling in."

"On call? What's that mean?"

"Any time the station is open, one of the employees or the staff volunteers must be present to make certain everything is looked after. You know, lights, telephones, whatever."

"Fine, Merlin, lead on."

"I was going to walk," he offered, locking the door behind, "but I'll get the car if you'd rather."

"No, I'll walk. Dare I ask if you're feeling better? Or will that bring on another cold shoulder?"

He didn't know what it was about this woman that made him bristle. Then he remembered Hattie's request that he look after Dusty—if it had been a request, if he hadn't been imagining the whole thing. He glared at her, then forced himself to answer.

"Yes. I apologize for my abruptness. As I'm sure you can understand, administering emergency procedure can be very risky. You can be sued if your results aren't acceptable."

She didn't answer. But she didn't believe for

one minute that this man would stop to worry about being sued before acting. No, it was something else that held him back. As for that weird story about the man with the beard, she was still working on that one.

Nick took a cigarette from his pocket and placed it between his lips.

"I'm surprised that you smoke. Most doctors don't approve."

"I don't. Approve, that is. But I don't give advice either—not anymore."

She watched him take two quick draws and stub the cigarette out. He didn't do it smoothly, not like a man who'd been a longtime indulger. "How long have you been smoking?"

"About a year, since the accident," he amended.

"The accident didn't do you in, so you're looking for another way? You have a death wish, do you?"

He didn't answer. Hell, he'd wrestled with that question too many hours with no clear answer.

"Let's just say that I don't care much what happens to me."

The flat acceptance in his voice was obvious. She felt a kind of tug deep inside, a response to his casual dismissal of concern.

"I know what you mean," she murmured. "There was a time when I first got out of jail that I went to the beach and stood looking out at the horizon. The waves lapped at my feet, riding higher and higher as the tide came in, burying my feet in the sand. I didn't want to move."

"Why did you?"

She gave an uneasy cough. "It was very strange. I heard Hattie's voice. She said that I couldn't do it. It was time for me to come home. And I did."

Nick knew that she was telling him something that she probably would never admit to anybody. He knew, and he understood.

"When did that happen, Dusty?"

"Two days before I came back."

The silence fell between them, deep and eerie. They shared some strange common thread that neither wanted to acknowledge, but neither wanted to break off.

Finally Nick kicked a discarded soda can, sending it across the street in a clatter. "Why were you in jail, Dusty?"

"I was a police officer accused of taking a bribe."

"I don't believe that!" he said.

"Doesn't matter," she said. "I did my time. It's over—in the past, behind me. This is now and now is whatever I decide to do."

"It's never over," he said. "I'm still doing my time."

She took a chance and glanced over at him. He was a thousand miles away. Pain had carried him there and held him in the netherworld where he was a prisoner.

"I think keeping yourself prisoner is the most binding of all. How long before you let yourself out of jail, put yourself on parole, Doctor Elliott?"

"I don't know," he said, reaching for another cigarette, then replacing the pack in his jacket pocket without opening it when he realized he was already holding one. "My now is still mixed up with the past."

"But you're the wizard. You can change that. You can change the future, too, according to Aunt Hattie."

"Only on the Orient Express," Nick said sadly, reaching the station door and opening it.

Dusty took a deep breath and stepped inside the shadowy reception area. She turned and, taking Nick's hand, redeemed an imaginary ticket. With the motions of a mime, she punched a hole in the ticket and handed it back to him.

"This isn't China, but the Stone Mountain Express is leaving any minute, sir. Welcome aboard."

"Perhaps you'd like to watch the other storytellers," Betty Hirt said. "Then, later, after you see what we're doing, we'll go over your part."

"Fine," Dusty agreed, slipping into a seat in

the small theater, high up in the darkness where she felt safe from prying eyes.

Nick had left her in Betty's hands and assumed his place at the reception area by the door. The other members of the ghost brigade arrived and, after being introduced to Dusty, murmured their condolences and began to chat among themselves. It was obvious that most of them had done this before. Only a few nervous first-timers hovered around the fringe area.

At last the lights dimmed, and one by one the story-tellers took the stage and began their tales. Each story was limited to five or six minutes and, as David Thomas explained, was the teller's own interpretation of the story they'd been given.

There was the salty old sea captain who, with his appearance and heavy brogue, invoked the sound and smell of the sea. His tale about the maiden who kept the light burning in the lighthouse to save her love was totally believable.

There was the elderly African American who told a slave tale of old, holding his lantern and speaking in dialect so perfect that Dusty felt as if she were in another time.

A tall dark-haired girl with a sad expression told of a revolutionary war hero who was beheaded and walked his post forever after without his head. And a Cajun, complete with accent, took the listeners to the pumpkin patch and scared them into never returning again.

"The story coming up is my favorite," Nick

said, sliding into the seat beside Dusty. "The teller is Betty Hirt's husband, and his is the last one on the tour."

Moments later a burly, jovial man launched into the tale of a circuit-riding preacher whose body was moved all over the swamp in an attempt to cover up his murder. It wasn't the story that was so entertaining, but the teller, who might have been Hattie's counterpart on any Broadway stage.

Applause broke out, then the lights came on and the participants, more relaxed now, began to plan their customary trek to the coffee shop for coffee and sweets.

"I have your script here, Dusty," Betty said, holding out a thin stack of papers. "Normally we ask you to read it and then return the script. Once read, you're expected to tell the story in your own words, in your own way. But we decided that wouldn't be fair to you since you didn't audition as a storyteller and time is so short."

"So, does that mean I can memorize it as is?"

Betty looked at David helplessly. "Normally we like you to make the story your own, but in this case we'll do whatever makes you more comfortable. Shall we go over the story now?"

Dusty looked at the others making preparations to leave and shook her head. "No, if that's what the others did, that's what I'll do. May I take it home with me and read it tonight?"

"Of course," David agreed. "Then we'll meet with you tomorrow afternoon and practice it at least once before we go to final rehearsal tomorrow night."

"Tomorrow night? But I don't know if I can learn it that soon."

"I'll help you," Nick said, standing up beside her.

"Fine," Betty agreed, glancing at her watch. "Now it's calorie time. Shall we adjourn to the coffee shop?"

"No, I don't think so," Dusty began, edging toward the door. "I think—"

She was going to decline, plead that she needed to read the script, but the words that finished her sentence weren't hers. They came from nowhere.

"I think—I'll go!" she said, then blinked in surprise.

"Fine with me," Nick agreed.

He hadn't expected her to go with the cast, but he hadn't expected her to agree to Hattie's request either. He wasn't sure whether he was pleased or disappointed.

As for Hattie's fortune, greed usually won, and he couldn't blame Dusty for taking the money. But somehow he had the feeling that Dusty wouldn't have decided on following Hattie's request for the money alone. Unless she had some kind of take-the-money-and-run plan in mind.

Moments later they were walking down the sidewalk and entering an artistically lit coffee house.

"How'd it go?" one customer asked.

"Dress rehearsal tomorrow night?" another questioned.

"Does everybody here know everybody else?" Dusty asked as she slid into the booth and Nick followed.

"This place is the chief hangout for all the artists and painters. So, yes, they pretty much know each other."

"And you? Are you part of the group?"

"No," he said, then thought about his answer for a moment. "Sometimes. When Hattie insisted on coming, and when she wasn't feeling well. I came with her."

The waitress took orders for drinks and snacks, her eyes straying back to Nick between each order, then on to Dusty with something close to animosity in her glance.

"Personal friend of yours?" Dusty asked when the woman walked away.

"Who?"

"The waitress."

"No. I don't have any personal women friends, not anymore."

"You cared about Hattie, didn't you?"

"Yes," he answered, but he didn't volunteer any more information.

David walked through the throng toward

their booth, taking the last available seat on the outside, forcing Nick to slide even closer to Dusty. He leaned out to speak around Nick. "We're really glad you're going to take Hattie's place and work with us at the Station. Hattie has been with us almost from the beginning."

"I don't know how much I'll be doing," Dusty said. "I'm no actress and I don't know a thing about the arts."

David took a long, interested look at Dusty before answering. "I think you're going to be surprised. Hattie always thought you had a terrific imagination. She said you used to make up your own plays, the two of you."

"She did?" Dusty felt uncomfortable with the constant reminders of Hattie's expectations. "I thought you didn't know anything about me."

"We didn't, not about Dusty. But she talked constantly about a little girl named Desirée. I thought Desirée was her own child, that she'd died," David said softly.

"Desirée did," Nick said. "But Dusty lives on."

Dusty was surprised by David's interest in her, but then she realized that he made everyone feel special. Still, she was glad to see the waitress bringing their drinks. She had the feeling that if Nick hadn't been pinned in, he would have fled. David's attention was eventually drawn to another table, and he stood and moved away. The other storytellers sitting in the booth began to talk about the upcoming dress rehearsal.

"Hattie was to wear a red satin ballgown," Nick said. "Complete with a hoop."

"I hope they don't expect me to do that. I probably can't walk in a hoop. My legs and feet always get tangled up in my bathrobe."

"Hattie said she felt like Scarlett O'Hara." Nick chuckled. "Truth is," he continued, "she was more like Miss Pittypat."

"I think I'd be more comfortable as Mammy."

Nick turned an odd look on her. "You know, in the new *Scarlett* book, Mammy was buried in that red petticoat."

"Are you threatening my life?" Dusty shivered, not from the thought of Nick making a threat, but from the heat of his gaze. He hadn't moved when David had left. They were still thigh to thigh, his arm planted along the back of the booth, creating a little hollow in which she was sitting.

He was surprised at the latent sexual desire she continued to feed in him. Sex was one of the things that he hadn't had much time for before the accident. All his energy had been concentrated on his career, on his reputation, on the specialized laser surgery that he'd helped pioneer and continued to develop.

Even his wife had given up. Their sex life had never been particularly intense, but she hadn't seemed to mind. As for Nick, she was available and their coupling didn't take energy away from his career. She probably would have been surprised to learn that there hadn't been others. As his wife, she'd always been there for him, and he'd thought little about her.

Until that last night. She'd accused him of being too tired to see what was happening and too full of his own importance to know when it was time to stop. It had taken one of his surgical assistants to send him home, to dismiss him from his own operating room, to take a chance on being ruined by the powerful Dr. Elliott when he demanded that Nick go home. Oh yes, he knew about threats. He took a long look at the woman beside him and realized in surprise that tonight he wasn't on the defensive.

"I never threaten anymore," he said softly.

"And I never wear red satin."

He shook off the feeling that they were being enclosed in some kind of bubble that closed off the conversation of the others. "Too bad, red is the color of your aura."

Dusty scoffed. "Auras, horoscopes, signs, I'd have thought a man like you would laugh at all that nonsense."

"I did. Once." Nick drained his coffee mug and stood. He didn't understand what he was doing there with this gypsy woman, or why she was chiseling away at the protective shell he'd constructed around himself. "If you're going to read your ghost story, we'd better go."

"You're right." She followed him from the restaurant, returning the generous good nights being issued by the cast. Their comfortable acceptance wasn't easy for Dusty. She felt as if she were being welcomed under false pretenses. "I wonder if they'd be so friendly if it weren't for Hattie's money?"

His surprise showed. "Why wouldn't they?"

"I guess I haven't got too many friends left. Prison has a way of making good-bye permanent. And suddenly you're alone and you don't know how it happened."

"Fate or by choice, the end results are the same. People find it easy to leave you alone if you push them away."

"From the looks you get when you step into the room, Merlin, I think any loneliness on your part is definitely through choice."

"And yours?"

"Through choice too."

"Is that normal for a police officer? I thought you had to be a team player."

Team. She felt a pain slice through her. "I had a partner once."

"Once? What happened?"

She waited a long time before answering. "We were answering a call. He was killed by a drug-crazed kid. It was my fault. I didn't follow procedure. I was so sure I could talk him down. My partner tried to save me."

"Is that why you went to jail? Pretty strong punishment, isn't it, for a bad judgment call?"

"No, that's how I got reassigned to a nice safe desk job that would keep me out of trouble and not put anybody else in danger."

Nick laughed. "Safe? Keep you out of trouble? Now, why don't I believe that?"

"Because there is no safe place, Merlin. You know it and I learned it. My nice safe job made me the fall guy in an organization that stole money from orphans and widows. After that I became the example to anybody else ready to blow the whistle. That's how I went to jail."

Nick stopped at the corner beneath the streetlight and took a long look at Dusty. He hadn't been able to get over the drastic change in her appearance. She wasn't the tough, hard-edged woman she'd been that first night. Wearing the skirt and shawl, she looked like a wild-eyed gypsy. His body still tingled where they'd touched, and his mind had done a fast reshuffling of his impression of her character.

"But you're innocent, aren't you?" he asked.

"Sure, but that conclusion and a dollar will get you a dozen stale doughnuts. What about you, magic man? Why are you still holed up here?"

He continued to study Dusty for a moment,

then turned and started walking toward the house.

"Don't want to bare your soul, huh? Doesn't matter. My last roommates were a lot more dangerous, and there were more of them."

"The accident," he finally said. "It left me with some other problems that I'm still dealing with my wife, Lois. And then there was Hattie."

"You didn't kill Lois, Nick," Dusty said, misunderstanding his statement. "It took me a long time, but I'm a good judge of people now. You loved her once."

"No," he admitted in a tight voice, "that's the hell of it. I didn't just kill her that night. I'd been doing it for years.

FIVE

The next morning there was a shiny black box tied with orange and black curly ribbons on the table by Dusty's bed.

Attached to the ribbon was an accordion folded tag which read: *Adopt-a-Ghost, an official souvenir of* A Tour of Southern Ghosts.

There were three pages of serious instructions which proclaimed that Dusty was the proud parent of an original Southern Ghost. The first panel instructed her to give her ghost a name. She moved on to the second page, but the smell of coffee interrupted her reading, and she quickly reached for her clothing, threading her long legs into the wrinkled jeans. This ghost must have been Merlin's idea; he could help choose a name.

She could almost hear her aunt's familiar "Tsk, tsk, tsk" as Dusty pulled a brush through her hair and caught it up in a butterfly clip. So she didn't look the way she had the night before; Nick would have to accept her as she really was, not as she was when she let Hattie's influence dictate her dress.

As she left the bedroom she picked up the box and her script. First she'd thank Nick for her gift. Then she'd read the damned script while she drank her morning coffee. The sooner she got the story down, the sooner she'd get over the feeling that Hattie was looking over her shoulder.

The kitchen was empty, but the coffee was warm and there were several boxes of cereal on the counter. She grinned at the selection: Monsters and Marshmallows, Crunchy Critters, and Nuts and Bolts. She would never have picked any one of them for the intense, dark-eyed man who was her roommate. It was hard to believe, but Aunt Hattie's wizard had a whimsical side.

As she ate the cereal, she finished reading the instructions for the care of her own private ghost. *Choose carefully where you place your ghost; they're often fussy if they don't like the spot.*

With a smile on her face she slid the ribbon away and lifted the top of the box. She was to leave the box open for twenty-four hours to allow the ghost to get acquainted with its new home. In the meantime, she rose and dutifully followed the instructions to drape the curly ribbon on the outside doorknob to announce the arrival of the ghost to the neighborhood.

In the box was a small canister marked Ghost Food. It too was to remain open during the night so that the ghost could feed. The canister would last for one year, from one *Tour of Southern Ghosts* to the next.

Dusty smiled. The idea for this souvenir had to have come from Hattie. Everything about it brought back memories of their pretend games from Dusty's childhood. Dusty blinked back the tears as new guilt overwhelmed her. She'd always thought there was time. Once she'd proved herself, she'd come back and say she was sorry. But she'd waited too long. How could everything have gone so wrong?

Swallowing back the tears, Dusty poured a fresh cup of coffee and settled down to read her script. She couldn't change the past, but she could do this last thing, tell the story.

The story, that of a woman who was married to a Confederate officer missing after the Battle of Shiloh, was terse and emotionless. The woman's children were grown and her slaves had disappeared one by one when she could no longer feed them, leaving her alone to protect her home and wait for her husband to return. When she refused to believe that he was dead, refused to move away with her friends, she was left alone. And every night she waited in the parlor for her man to return.

"Fool woman!" Dusty said as the back door opened and a sweat-streaked Nick Elliott entered.

"Who's a fool?"

"The woman in this story, waiting night after night for a man who is dead. Why didn't she get on with her life? There must have been somebody who would help her."

Nick could have compared the woman in the story to both himself and Dusty, except she didn't have Hattie.

"I don't think Hattie had worked out that part of the story. She was still working on the ending when she died."

Dusty laid the paper down and took a good look at Nick Elliott. He was wearing a black T-shirt over the kind of latex running pants that covered the entire lower body like the skin, and exposed every part of the male anatomy. She gulped.

The accident might have left Merlin with some kind of mysterious wound that wasn't obvious, but there was at least one part of him that was very obvious, or as obvious as it could be, encased in latex.

His hair, held back by a teal blue band, was damp, feathering over the band and giving an untidy sensual look to a face that seemed to burn with intensity.

"You've been running?" Her voice sounded tight.

Nick gave a dry laugh. "Running? Me? I've been doing my usual slow shuffle through the neighborhood."

"I've seen lots of athletes wear running gear like that, but never up close. I especially like the lightning bolt down the sides."

He wiped his face with a thick towel and reached for the juice carton in the refrigerator. "What's the matter, wild woman, are my masculine charms getting to you?"

"Of course not!" she snapped. "I just don't want you disturbing my ghost."

He dropped the towel and turned, a look of cautious disbelief on his face. "Your ghost?"

"The one you left in the box on my table last night."

"Sorry, but I didn't leave anything in your room last night." He could have admitted that he had been in her room sometime during the night. But he still wasn't certain if he'd stood at the foot of her bed and stared at her in the moonlight, or if he'd been dreaming. The one thing he did know was that in his dream she'd had the same effect on him as her silver-blue eyes were having on him now. Latex was hell on body parts. Desire was hell on control.

"Well, somebody did. I've got the box to prove it."

She was serious.

He wasn't concentrating on the box, but on the thought of being in her room.

"I'll shower and then you can tell me about your ghost," he said, and, carrying the towel strategically, moved past the table and into the hallway. Climbing the stairs was as painful as usual, but this time the accident wounds took second place to another kind of pain.

Dusty watched him climb the stairs. He might claim his innocence, but she'd seen the box. She'd discovered his weird collection of cereal, and she'd seen the lightning bolt on his running gear.

A grin slipped out. She was getting to the ice man. That knowledge made the warm spot in her stomach bounce around, touching the nerve endings with heat. She didn't know about all that nonsense he'd spouted the previous night about not loving his wife, but she'd be willing to give odds that the woman had loved Nick. As for murder, that was some kind of hair shirt he'd wrapped himself in.

Penance or punishment.

By the time she heard the water running overhead, she decided that maybe a cold shower was the right idea.

She sighed and forced herself to relax. It had been a long time since she'd been with a man, even longer since she'd felt such an attraction. Hattie might have been eccentric as hell, but her taste in men was primeval.

Dusty refilled her coffee cup and listened as the shower finally stopped. Out the kitchen window she caught sight of the tree house and thought about the first night she'd come, when she'd tackled Nick as an intruder. The shiver she was fighting turned into a tremor that would have registered at least a five on the Richter scale.

Turning back to the table, Dusty fingered the script. "Wow! This isn't supposed to be part of the bargain, Hattie. I have about as much future with Merlin as I have as a police officer. This house-sharing deal was not a smart move on your part."

The black box on the table suddenly shivered and slid toward the edge, where it teetered for a moment until Dusty caught it. She blotted up the smear of coffee she must have spilled beneath it.

"Sorry, Siggy," she said. "I'll find you a safer place."

"Siggy?" Nick was standing in the doorway looking around. "Is he here?"

"How the hell would I know? The thing about a ghost is that you can't see him, or it. At least I can't. You want to look?"

Nick stared at Dusty, catching sight of the black box she was holding. It was filled with a nest of excelsior in which a small empty canister was nestled. "What's that?"

"Siggy. My ghost. The one you left on my table."

"I promise you, I didn't leave anything on your table. I don't know how he got there. Why'd you name him Siggy?"

"I don't know. It just came to me. Maybe because this whole thing has Freudian overtones. I guess it got to me subliminally. Sigmund Freud seemed appropriate. You got a better idea?"

"Yeah, call her Eve, as in the many faces of Eve. I think we're both nuts. Maybe Hattie was smarter than either of us knew."

Dusty lifted her mug again. The coffee was cold, but she clasped the cup to keep her hands still. "How's that?"

"We're both misfits, dropouts, wounded beings that ought to be locked up together. We're each other's punishment."

"I'll buy that," she said, turning to put the cup in the sink. "The problem I have is the together part."

She didn't know how she managed to drop the cup, nor how it came to nick a slice from her finger. But suddenly bright drops of blood were dripping into the sink.

Then Nick was there, holding her hand, running cold water over it, then blotting it with a towel. "Let's get upstairs to the bathroom," he said sternly. "You need antibiotic ointment and a bandage."

Moments later they were wedged in the tiny bathroom, still steamy from Nick's shower, with

Nick covering her finger with ointment and deftly applying a bandage.

"Wow, that looks spiffy, Doc," Dusty said, trying unsuccessfully to move away and succeeding only in wedging them even more tightly together. "You're very efficient."

"I aim to please," he said, his voice low and hoarse.

"I'll bet you aren't used to operating in such small spaces," she whispered.

"I don't—" *operate at all*, he started to say, then realized what he'd done. Applying a simple bandage to a cut finger didn't seem like much, but he'd reacted instinctively, an action that he would never have made a few days earlier. A simple cut finger had become more significant than surgery.

"Don't what?" Dusty prompted.

He took in a deep breath, allowing the very female scent of her to fill his nostrils, and he felt the sudden surge of adrenaline in response.

"Don't . . ." But he couldn't remember what he'd started to say. All he could see was the wild beauty of the woman who looked up at him with trust in her eyes and mischief in her smile.

"Neither do I," she said, "not normally."

"But there's nothing about this situation that's normal, is it?"

"Not for me," she managed to say, despite the fact that her throat was practically closed off by the lump that grew bigger by the second. She hadn't felt so tongue-tied since she'd walked across the stage to receive her badge at the police academy.

He touched her hair, allowing his fingers to tangle in the long silver strands that cascaded down her back. "I've never seen hair quite this color. I'll bet you were really a hit with the criminal element."

"There was a time or two that it could have been pretty tempting to break the law instead of enforcing it. What about you? I'll bet every female patient you had automatically disrobed when they caught sight of you."

"Would you?"

Her mind suddenly pictured the two of them nude together. "Would you want me to?"

"I don't know. I don't understand what's happening here, and I don't think I like it."

There was suddenly no oxygen in the air. Dusty felt as if she were smothering. His dark eyes devoured her, swallowing up all her fears and turning them into wonder. She was shy. She was afraid. She was trembling.

His gaze roamed over her, searing her with heat and anger. He was right, he didn't like what was happening. But he couldn't stop it any more than she could.

"Sweet Jesus," she whispered, struggling with her confusion.

"Ah, hell!" he swore, and kissed her. For a

few seconds they both sailed over the edge of reality.

Then he was gone.

For the rest of the morning, Dusty read her script and tried to improvise an ending. She could do this, she reasoned. Once, long ago, she and Hattie had made up plays and performed skits. She remembered the times with such affection. But now, the ideas wouldn't come.

Years of street life and crime had killed the creative juices. Though, she admitted with chagrin, they hadn't stifled the physical ones.

That was the problem, she reasoned. Being in the house with Nick was messing up her mind. Technically he wasn't even in the house now, but she felt his presence there. She also felt the ache in her lower body and grimaced. The situation wasn't any easier for him. He'd kissed her. Lordy, how he'd kissed her. And she'd returned that kiss. But when his body hardened against her and his hand had found her breast, she'd cried out in protest.

Moments later she'd been alone in the bathroom, with the sound of a sigh of disappointment heavy in the air. Had it been Nick who'd voiced his displeasure without knowing? Or had —had she imagined it?

This was getting heavy. What they both had to do was face it and get past it. First they had to identify the "it." If she was reading the situation right, Dr. Nick Elliott was as horny as a stallion in sniffing distance of a mare in heat. She was suffering from pure lust for a man who was a writhing mass of contradictions. They were heading for a collision unless she found a way to defuse the situation.

But how?

She couldn't leave, at least not immediately. Her probation prohibited that. What she didn't understand was why he didn't leave. He'd been sent there to torment her. He was her punishment. If he had been an entertainer, he'd be the kind of man who could step on a stage and mesmerize the audience with his dramatic good looks.

Why was he staying?

Maybe he wasn't as well-off as he'd said. He said he was rich, but he'd been in an accident that must have cost a small fortune. He'd said he'd make arrangements to buy her out. Arrangements?

She dropped her script and let her mind run free. Then it came to her. He might not have money left, but according to Hattie's attorney, Dusty did. She'd buy out his interest in the house. That would solve the problem of too much togetherness. With a nod of satisfaction she picked up the script and began to read again.

She was beginning to formulate another idea about the story when there was a resounding thud. Glancing up, she couldn't see any reason for the noise.

Then she saw it, the box containing her ghost was upset on the floor, the excelsior scattered. As she watched, the ghost food canister suddenly flipped over on its side and began to roll across the floor, coming to a stop at Dusty's feet.

This was too much. She'd loved the whimsical instructions on the card that came with the box. Choose the place where you place the box carefully, it had said. If the ghost isn't happy it may show its displeasure, it warned. But this was testing her credibility.

First the growing tension between her and Nick.

Then the mysterious sighs and unexplainable incidents.

Hattie's house was a seething mass of undercurrents, and Dusty had learned the hard way that the only thing she could believe was what she saw, heard, felt, and tasted with her own senses.

The nonsense she'd spouted about Merlin the wizard was just that—nonsense. Nick's suggestion that Hattie might come back as a ghost was just as ridiculous. All of this had to be happening because of the tension between her and Nick.

In spite of her resolve to study the script, her mind went back to Nick. She made a mental list of possible solutions if he refused to sell. Discuss "it." Bring the volatile situation into the open. Admit to "it." Force a confrontation and get past the lust.

The lid on the floor vibrated.

Dusty grabbed her script and her coat and left the house in a jog. She didn't know where Nick was, but there was the sound of laughter in the air as she ran toward the ART Station.

Nick stood at the hospital window, trying to explain what had happened in the last few days. Bill Lewis, the doctor who had seen him through the accident and the trauma afterward, didn't interrupt.

"I know that bandaging a finger is nothing, but I did it, Bill. And I didn't need to be asked. As for the incident in the restaurant, I can't explain it. If anybody else on the hospital board heard me saying that Sigmund Freud was there, they'd ship me off to the loony bin."

"You've known all along, Nick, that your memory loss is selective. Anything to do with medicine, you closed out. I can't say that I understand why you made your work the scapegoat for the death of your wife, but who ever understands the way the mind operates?"

"It was more than just her death," he said. "It was the way I cheated her, from the beginning."

"Well, I'm glad you're feeling better about

things. I was afraid that when Hattie died you'd go into a tailspin."

"No. In some strange kind of way, her death was a catharsis. Then Dusty came along . . ."

Bill stood from behind his desk and flipped on the X-ray viewer on the wall behind him. "Say, Nick. I wish you'd have a look at this and tell me what you think."

Nick turned and looked at the film being displayed. He studied it for a long moment, almost unaware of his mind cataloging the chest and the mass that filled the picture. It was huge, and it was a puzzle, totally unlike anything he'd ever seen.

"How old is the patient?"

"Twenty-nine weeks old," Bill answered, afraid to verbalize Nick's involvement. He knew that memory return could be a fragile thing, and he waited.

"You're kidding," Nick said sternly. "A fetus? What did the autopsy show?"

"She isn't dead, at least not yet. But she's in trouble. We're considering surgery."

"Now?"

"Two doctors in California are doing some remarkable work while the fetus is still in the womb. Of four cases they've attempted, three have been successful."

"Of course, it would depend on the problem," Nick said, leaning forward for a closer view. "You might be able to use laser on something like this."

Moments later Nick had projected a possible method of removing the mass. So engrossed was he in the problem that it took him by surprise when Bill made his offer. "If the board decides to approve our attempt, do you want to assist?"

"Yes! I mean . . ." His voice trailed off. "No. I'll never go back to that. I made up my mind. Don't—don't do this to me, Bill."

"You can't hide from what you are forever, Nick. The mind may have given you a respite, but it's not going to tolerate your refusal to be what you are. I don't know what you expect to do with the rest of your life, but I think it's time you gave it some serious thought, and if it takes Sigmund Freud to force you, I say welcome."

"Not Sigmund Freud," Nick said in a low voice as he started toward the door. "Hattie started it by sending me an ex-convict who's driving me crazy."

"So call the police. I'm sure the law can get rid of whoever is harassing you."

Nick gave a dry laugh. "You don't understand, Bill. The woman *is* a cop."

Bill shook his head. "I don't have any idea what you're talking about, but if it involves fending off a woman, you, of all people in the world, ought to be able to handle it."

On the way home Nick considered Bill's words. He couldn't hold back the return of his memory. It came with a rush as unstoppable as the flood of water breaking through a dam and overwhelming everything in its path. He was still a doctor. He couldn't deny that. He just couldn't deal with it yet either.

One thing he could deal with was Dusty O'Brian. He'd never believed his jest that Hattie was likely to come back as a ghost. It had just slipped out, a tool to deal with the pragmatic approach to life of Hattie's adopted niece. He refused to believe in ghosts.

Dusty was another story. At least she was flesh and blood, a human being, a problem he could face. Sure, he was attracted to her. Any man with even half a dose of testosterone would be attracted to that body, those eyes, that hair.

She'd charged in, determined to run her own show. On the defensive, it was her mouth that had fueled the problem until she'd learned of Hattie's death. She still thought she'd closed off her past. But now, like him, she was discovering that there were cracks in her coat of armor, beginning with the storytelling and the gypsy skirt.

Just thinking about the kiss they'd shared made him hard, about how her lips parted hungrily beneath his, joining in that same surge of raw need. It was Hattie who had brought Dusty to him, but it was Desirée who had unthawed Nick and freed his inhibitions, released his cravings.

That had to stop. As he'd so often advised his

patients concerned about losing weight: If they craved a thing so much that it interfered with reason, indulge it and get past the need.

Indulge the craving.

Sound advice.

He'd make love to Dusty and satisfy that need. Afterward he'd decide what he would do about her, about his medical practice, and his life.

"And don't you interfere, Hattie Lanier," he said out loud, startling one of the homeless standing on the street corner as he passed. "I've decided to take back my life and put the past behind me."

"Jolly good idea!" the man said with a smile of approval.

When Nick turned back to hand him a buck, the man had disappeared around the corner. A quick breeze, funneled by the buildings, caught the bill, jerked it from Nick's hand, and carried it away.

Nick felt an odd sense of anticipation sweep over him. He felt like that bill, caught up in movement, being swept along to some new place.

He might, he decided brashly, take a trip, maybe on the Orient Express. He rather liked the idea of being a mysterious character, alone, riding through the night to nowhere.

But perhaps that's what he'd been.

SIX

Betty welcomed Dusty into her office, cleared off the only chair, and motioned for her to have a seat.

"Howdy, Dusty, what's wrong?"

"I've been studying the script this morning and I—I confess, I haven't any idea what I'm doing. There's no ending."

"Let me see it." Betty took the typewritten copy and flipped to the end. "Good heavens, where's the rest?"

"I don't know. That's all I have. Nick said that Hattie changed the ending from year to year. That she hadn't decided this year what she'd do."

Betty frowned. "That's true. But the original story had an ending. As I recall, the woman became ill, and as she lay dying, her husband returned. They were finally reunited, but it took death to accomplish it."

A shiver ran down Dusty's backbone. "Doesn't sound like the kind of story Hattie would tell. She liked happy endings."

"Yes, that was her dilemma. She always wanted to fix things, make them right. Let me look around and see if I can't find something written down in our files. In the meantime, would you like to get the feel of telling? You could rehearse what you have in the theater."

"On the stage?"

"Don't worry. There's nobody in the building but you and me. You can be as bad or as hammy as you like."

Reluctantly Dusty let herself be walked to the theater. Betty turned on a soft spotlight that filled a circle on the platform and left Dusty to the empty stage.

"Once upon a time—" she began. "No, dummy, that's a fairy tale. This is for adults. All right, you people, listen up. No. That won't work."

Dusty closed her eyes and let her mind wander back to a time long lost in the recesses of her mind. She'd been eleven and standing on the back porch. On her head was a crown and in her hand a scepter with a star on the end.

"Now, Dusty, close your eyes and let your spirit float free," Aunt Hattie was saying. "You're not a little girl anymore. You're a queen. Stand straight and feel like a queen."

"But I feel silly," she'd argued.

"Of course you do. You're not ready yet. Just stand there. It will come. Open your mind and your heart. You're whatever you want to be. You just have to let yourself feel it. Feel like a queen."

Dusty found herself remembering that little girl, remembering how Hattie had made her let go of what she was in order to become whatever she imagined. And she closed her eyes, emptying her mind, waiting for her mind to be ready.

Suddenly she wasn't on a stage any longer; she was at the window of the plantation house, peering into the fading shadows of the night sky. She was cold and hungry. In the distance there was the sound of cannon fire and the smell of smoke. Everything else was quiet.

"You have to close your eyes," she whispered to her imaginary audience. "Free your mind of the real world as you know it so that you can become a woman who lived a hundred and thirty years ago. She's afraid, very afraid. She's alone. The man she loves is gone and she wants him home, desperately. Feel her desperation."

And Dusty went on, describing the woman, how she felt, what she wanted, and where she was. Then Dusty felt the woman's pain. It was so acute that she broke off her tale and opened her eyes.

"Very good. Very powerful," Betty said in a hushed voice from the doorway. "I didn't understand Hattie's request that you tell her story, but you're going to be special."

"But I still don't know how it ends," Dusty said, trying to cover the eerie feeling that had swept over her.

"Well, I have two other versions of the same story here. Hattie said a relative composed this story originally and it was passed on to her. The woman's dead now, but Hattie had her permission to alter it any way she wanted."

Dusty took the folder Betty was holding. "I'll read them over, but I don't make any promises. This feels weird."

"Well, all you have to do is try. If you're terrible, nobody will hold it against you. The ART Station owes Hattie a great deal. Following her wishes is more important to the station than your performance. Don't forget, rehearsal tonight is at seven o'clock at the plantation house. Come early so that you can try on your costume."

"Can I bum a ride with somebody?"

"Don't worry, Nick will bring you. He attends all the rehearsals."

"But . . ."

The phone rang and Betty turned back to the office. Dusty left the stage and switched off the lights. She didn't know why she kept fighting. It was obvious that Hattie had set off a chain of events that she wasn't going to change. She might as well get on with fulfilling Hattie's request.

She could tell a story. She could deal with Nick. Hattie's plans for them to share the house were odd but workable. The only thing that Hattie couldn't have foreseen was the chemistry between Dusty and Merlin. The more she experienced it, the more certain she was that her plan to make love to the good doctor, get that settled, and offer to buy him out, was the answer.

Though Dusty had made her decision, she didn't have her inheritance yet. And she couldn't get it until she fulfilled her part of Hattie's request. For that she had to tell her story and become the ART Station's new mentor.

"Hah!" Some mentor. She didn't even have pocket money. Maybe a call to old J.R., Hattie's attorney, would provide that. Surely her promise to comply with Hattie's request would be good for a few bucks.

Back at Hattie's house she found the card J.R. had left, and she called him. After she stumbled through her explanation, he agreed to drop by the house and leave her a small advance on her inheritance.

After checking on Siggy, Dusty made herself a peanut butter and jelly sandwich and climbed into the tree house, where she read through the alternate endings. Hattie's solutions were very different, though in each the husband reappeared as a ghost.

"I don't know about this, Hattie. I don't think an authentic live woman would settle for a spirit. I mean, the illusion might be okay in the movies, but I'd want the real thing in my bed."

Nick entered the garden in time to hear the last half of her sentence. Dusty wanted a real man in her bed. As opposed to what? A scarred, wounded man? Him?

There was an ominous creak overhead as the wood protested Dusty's weight. "Dusty, you'd better come down. That tree house wasn't built as quarters for an adult."

"Oh, yes it was. Hattie and I both sat up here."

"Sure, years ago. Come down before it collapses."

She might have argued, just on general principle, except for the slight shift of the board on which she was sitting.

"All right. I might as well. I can't find a proper finish for this story anyway. The captain ends up dead. I like my men alive." She reached for the last board, the bottom rung on the foothold ladder.

It gave way.

She slipped, falling against Nick, who'd come to her aid. Both went tumbling to the ground. He was on his back, his arms automatically encircling her to protect her and to anchor himself.

As they fell he realized that his hands were on her breasts—full, unfettered breasts that molded themselves to him as he tried to move away. Her bottom fitted neatly against him, straddling the intrusive part of him that would have been embarrassingly obvious had she fallen on her stomach. She shifted her bottom, calling attention to his situation and her knowledge of it.

"Well, well. Guess Merlin doesn't care whether it's a bed or the ground."

He let out a muffled groan. "Don't push it, wildcat," he said in a harsh voice. "I feel your heart beating like that of a wounded bird caught in a net. My desire might be more visible, but yours is no less powerful."

To prove his point, he slid his hands beneath her shirt and found her nipples, rolling them between his fingertips. She gave a little cry and twisted herself away, sliding to her side, catching her weight on one elbow so that she could raise herself up and examine him.

"Are you hurt?" she asked.

"Hurt? Why? Are you offering to kiss my hurt and make it well?"

"I'm concerned, Merlin. I wouldn't want to think that I caused you any pain."

"There's always pain, Dusty. You can't possibly cause me any more than I've already felt."

"There it is again, that hair shirt you wear. Do you enjoy punishing yourself? I'm the one who fell on you."

"Not your fault," he protested. "I was—distracted."

"I shouldn't have distracted you."

"You didn't."

She smiled. He might claim that she wasn't the cause of his problem, but his body wasn't having any part of that idea. She waited. He wasn't making any effort to move, and though she had to find a way to get past their attraction to each other, nowhere was it written that she couldn't have a bit of fun at the same time.

"Where exactly are you hurt?" She ran her fingertips beneath his shirt and began to examine him with soft feathery motions designed to tease him. "Here?"

For a moment he stopped breathing. The wench. She was going to drive him crazy. The nerve endings in his skin bunched into hard, quivery knots that jerked beneath her touch. Moving lower, she reached the button at the waistband of his jeans. Before he knew what she was doing, it was open and her fingers were inching downward.

"Or maybe here?"

He reached out, clasping her arms with hands of steel, and jerked her forward so that she was lying over him.

"Did I find the spot?"

"You keep looking and you're going to find more than you can handle, Ms. Desirée O'Brian. Don't push me."

"Oh, was I pushing?"

This time he did push, moving her away as he came to his feet and walked to the porch. He didn't bother to fasten his jeans. She could see the waistband loose, exposing the black knit band of his briefs. He was tall and lean and gorgeous.

And she was left awash in the most powerful surge of sexual desire she'd ever known. The seduction of Nick Elliott was looming even more important than ever, and just as impossible.

Finally she stood and followed him.

Inside the kitchen he was standing at the sink, looking out the window. "You don't want this, Dusty," he said. "You really don't."

"Don't tell me what I want, Nick. I recognize the attraction, and I'm willing to admit it. Are you?"

"How long has it been since you've had a man make love to you?"

She watched as he turned to face her, his gaze pinning her down, forcing an answer. "Almost three years. Why? Do I have to pass some kind of test to qualify?"

"It's been almost two years since I've made love to a woman, and I don't think either of us is in a position to make a rational decision."

"Why is that, Merlin? I think I'd like an answer to why I can't make a decision about the men I sleep with."

"Go upstairs and get ready to go to rehearsal, Dusty. And don't take this any further."

"Why? Can't you handle the job?"

His lips curled into a smile, and his voice dropped to a thick whisper. "I can give you what you want, Dusty, but I think it would be a mistake."

"Why? Don't you think we can live together, cohabit, as the case may be? After all, we share the house, why shouldn't we share a bed? It would make things much simpler, wouldn't it? I'd call it a satisfying resolution to a problem that is readily apparent."

"Sharing a bed and a house with a woman isn't an answer," Nick said. "I know. I've already been there. It destroys the very thing you share. No matter how much desire you have for a person, it eventually dies and you're left with nothing. I won't do that to another woman, ever again."

"Whoa, magic man. I'm not talking about promises of forever; in fact, I had something much less permanent in mind."

"Oh, are we talking about a one-night stand here?"

"Something like that."

"To what purpose?"

"Sex, Merlin. Pure and simple sex. We use each other now, then we settle the details."

He winced. "That's what I'm not interested in."

She didn't understand the pain on his face. "I didn't mean between us. I thought I'd make it simple for you. I mean, I'm stuck here and so are you, for the moment. Let's not fight it. Later, when we can work it out, we'll go our separate ways."

"So you aren't looking for forever. You'll just use me for a while, then you'll move on? Isn't that a little cold?"

She looked at the bulge in his jeans and took a deep breath. "Cold? I don't think so, Merlin. I don't think cold is part of the problem."

"You're right. I want you. And I could sleep with you and give us both a temporary reprieve, but I've been down that road once. You've been lonely, been through a terrible ordeal, and I'm available. Hattie has somehow put her stamp of approval on me and that makes everything all right. But I won't be responsible for hurting you."

Dusty decided that there was a humming in the air around them. Almost as if they were generating sound with the heat that arced between their bodies.

"You're right," she finally said. "Hattie set this up, at least she tried. But, come on, she had no way of knowing that I'd really come back. So we can't blame this on her. If we did that, you'd have to admit that she also put her stamp of approval on me."

"Oh, Hattie brought you here all right," he

agreed. "I don't pretend to understand how or why, but I can see her hand in all this. Hell, I don't know why I'm refusing you. It's been a long time since somebody has begged me to go to bed."

"I'm not begging you, Nick Elliott."

But she had been, and that hurt. She'd lost sight of her original plan in the face of her desire. She wanted the man, wanted him in her bed, wanted his hot, sweaty body against hers. She wasn't used to being turned down either. She tried to salvage her pride.

"In fact," she snapped, "I've changed my mind. I don't want you in my bed. I was teasing you. You know about women who tease, don't you?"

"I know, and you weren't teasing. I don't think you're that kind of woman, Dusty. Whatever you do, you do it openly without apology."

"That's not what the prosecutor said at my trial. He claimed that I was a deceitful woman, lying, hiding my part in the crime. And everybody believed him."

Nick dropped his tough bravado act and took a step forward. "I don't. I believe you, Dusty. Why didn't you stay and fight instead of running away?"

"I'm not good at defending myself. I'm better at running."

"If you were innocent, you should have stayed and proved it."

"I was tired and it didn't matter anymore. The past is gone and my life and my criminal record with it. All I wanted was to shut that door and find some peace."

"I guess I can understand that, wildcat. But I won't compromise you or me, no matter how hard it is for me to keep my hands off you. Go get ready, Dusty, we have to go."

"All right," she agreed in a shaky voice, "but there's one thing I want to know. What are you afraid of, Merlin?"

"Maybe of being forced to answer that question, wildcat. Maybe of acknowledging that there is a future to face."

David met them at the gate. He sent Nick to check on the placement of the Halloween pumpkins they were arranging around the plantation, and escorted Dusty to the little house they were using for the wardrobe room.

Hattie's red dress was too large. The wardrobe mistress finally came up with a cream-colored ballgown trimmed with blue roses and lace.

"I never saw this before. Someone must have donated it. It's more elegant than anything we ordinally use, but we don't have time to sew a whole new gown. If it fits, we'll use it."

"The spook seekers won't care," David said.

"And it will be nice to have a beautiful woman in the house."

Two garments slipped from their hangers and fell to the floor, followed by a hat box that bounced directly on David's head.

He glanced around uneasily. "No offense intended. All the women on the tour are beautiful. It's just that this is the first time we've had a woman with silver hair involved. Maybe we should arrange some special light to set her off. No, being in the shadows is better."

He left, muttering to himself about the staging of Dusty's story. The wardrobe mistress managed to pin the dress to fit, cautioning Dusty not to lean over at the risk of being stuck.

"What do you mean? I have to wear this tonight at rehearsal?"

"Oh, yes. We always rehearse in costume. You have to learn how much freedom you have to move around. Don't worry, all the others are already dressed. You'd better get to the house. Oh, and take this lantern. All the tellers carry one."

Dusty found herself being pushed out the door, left alone to find her way to the house in the darkness by the light of a lantern.

As she walked down the sidewalk, she passed the first station, a large magnolia tree where the elderly man was embellishing on his tale. There were several people listening, people she didn't recognize.

"Damn." She didn't know she was going to have an audience.

"Now, now, Ms. Desirée, that's no language for a Confederate widow to use." Nick appeared at her side, a sleek silhouette with dark hair and dark lashes that made his face look like he should have been one of the participants.

"You almost scared me to death!" she said uneasily.

"You don't look dead. You look like a bride. Where'd they find that dress?"

"I don't know. The wardrobe mistress hadn't seen it before either. Apparently somebody donated it." She passed a prickly bush and took a step closer to Nick to avoid it, causing the skirt to fly up on the opposite side. "I don't know how any woman ever managed a hoop."

"Your character was a very special woman. At least according to Hattie. She waited for the man she loved, even when she knew he was probably dead."

They reached the house and Nick gallantly took her arm as they climbed the steps. "You're going to stand beneath the portrait?"

"Wherever it's the darkest."

He unhooked the velvet rope closing off the double doorway and allowed her to enter. She felt a sudden chill inside the room.

"This is spooky, Merlin. I feel as if somebody is watching."

"Maybe it's the woman in the painting."

Dusty took a step closer and looked up at the picture. On either side of the mantle were sconces holding candles with delicate flame-shaped bulbs that looked like real fire. They cast a ghostly light across the woman's face, partially shielding it from view. The odd thing was that now she appeared to have light-colored hair like Dusty's.

"What's that on her hair?" she asked.

"Looks like some kind of net. If I remember right, Scarlett, or maybe it was Melanie, wore one in *Gone With the Wind*."

"I've heard of pictures where the eyes seem to be following you no matter where you stand, but this is the first time I've seen one. At least her eyes aren't blue."

Nick studied the portrait. "I don't know. It's hard to tell in this light. They could be any color. But you're right. You get the feeling that she's watching us."

Dusty let out a concerned laugh. "First she falls on us, now she's watching. That's spooky. What happens now?"

"Get ready for your first audience," he said. "I hear them coming."

"You aren't going, are you?" She hadn't meant to sound so anxious, but she admitted to a certain amount of panic at being left alone.

"I suppose I could stand over here, in the corner, if that would make you feel better. I don't think I can be seen."

"Thank you, Merlin. I need all the help I can get."

Betty Hirt, followed by several volunteers, stepped into the doorway. "Oh, you look wonderful," she said. "Where'd that dress come from?"

Dusty explained once more that nobody seemed to know.

"Well, it's a cinch it's been packed up somewhere," Betty said, walking around Dusty. "The folds are still visible. And that fabric. It isn't something cheap that we'd buy for a costume."

"So, I'm wearing a plantation original!" Dusty didn't mean to sound so sharp, but she was getting the jitters big time.

"Well, you look lovely," someone in the back said.

"So, let's begin, shall we?" David joined the group and stood smiling encouragingly.

Dusty took a deep breath and closed her eyes. As she had in the theater, she instructed her onlookers to close their eyes also. "Allow the spirit world to merge with your inner being. We are in a plantation house just outside Atlanta. The Confederate forces are being driven back."

She wrung her hands anxiously. "I am here, alone in my house, waiting for the man I love to come back to me. I'm so afraid."

The light in the room was eerie, almost as if it were really being cast by candles, catching the uneasy currents of air and moving across the wall in smears of shadows.

Dusty finally opened her eyes and turned slightly, as if she'd heard someone call her. She hushed for a second and allowed herself to find Nick. The way he was standing, she could see the scar on his face. Odd, she hadn't noticed it that much. He always seemed to turn away from her so that side of his face was concealed. To-night it was a dark jagged mark that seemed more pronounced.

She noted the scar, but it didn't disturb her. She went on, speaking softly as the widow told of her love for the man who'd left her to fight in the war.

Her voice slowed, changed, became softer, more Southern. "Do you hear it? A horse's hooves outside?" she said, hurrying to the win-dow, then turning back in disappointment.

Nick listened, caught up in the reality she was creating with her words and the outpouring of emotion. Where the other tellers had a story, with stopping places where they alternately scared and made the listeners laugh, Dusty was simply creating a place and a time that had long passed. When she spoke of horses approaching, you could almost hear them. When she lowered her gaze in disappointment, there were tears in her eyes.

And through it all, the room enhanced and

fed the mood. The picture seemed to have more definition, and the silence deepened.

Then Dusty stopped.

"I'm sorry," she said. "I don't know where I'm going now. I reach this point and I feel as if I ought to move out of the room and into the hall-way."

"That wouldn't be smart," David said. "The children would be all over you. I think you'd lose the sense of illusion you're creating."

"I agree," Betty said. "Don't worry. This is just fine. You work on it some more, and we'll try again tomorrow night. You'll become more confident as you go."

Dusty nodded. But she wasn't at all sure about tomorrow night. She was still having trouble with the kind of ending she was seeing in her mind. She was drawn to the stairs. Somehow she knew there was a place up there where the woman in her story wanted to go. She wasn't meant to wait here, in this room, but somewhere else.

The tour moved on, with Betty inviting Dusty to join them to see the last story, which would be told on the lawn in front of the house.

Dusty didn't respond. She stood, moving her head from side to side like some kind of antenna, trying to focus on the source of her concern.

Nick came forward. "What's wrong?"

"I don't know. What's upstairs, Nick?"

"Two storage rooms and a corridor."

"No, that isn't it. What else?"

He frowned. "I don't know. They're locked, with a chain and padlock. I've never been inside. Is it important?"

"No. That's all right." When he took her arm this time, she let him, leaning against him as if she were cold and sought the warmth of his body.

"Are you too cool?" He stopped and pulled her close, folding his arms around her.

"Yes. I mean no. I guess it must be this place. It's got me spooked big time."

"Sorry, I don't have a coat, but there's hot apple cider in the food tent."

She laid her head against his chest and pressed closer. "I think I need you to hold me for a minute," she said. "If you don't mind."

He didn't.

In fact, as he had every time she'd gotten close to him, he ended up holding her. But this time he was determined not to let it go further. When she leaned back and looked up at him, he smothered the thought of her lips and how inviting they were. He'd only allowed himself to move a little closer. He wouldn't do anything more than give her a gentle kiss of comfort.

Her eyes were dazed, almost sleepy, trusting. She lifted her mouth willingly, wrapping her arms tighter around his waist, pressing her breasts against him. Nothing on earth could have stopped them.

Nothing on earth did.

As their lips met, the smell of honeysuckle swept down the hallway from the second floor. At the sound of footsteps descending the stairs, Nick pulled away.

"What's wrong, Nick?"

"There can't be anyone up there," he said, tucking her in the curve of his shoulder as he stared up into the darkness.

"Let's get out of here, Merlin. This kind of spell is too much, even for a magic man."

They left the house, catching up with the group watching the last storyteller. As they stood in the yard listening to the tale of a body that kept coming back to life, Dusty turned and glanced up at the house.

The windows on the top floor were dark. Then for a moment she thought she saw a faint light silhouetting the shadow of a woman, a woman watching.

A woman with silver hair.

SEVEN

Dusty changed into her regular clothing and met Nick at his car. She was caught up in a strange mood of shifting emotions. His presence had been the only thing that had kept her in that parlor tonight. Yet that same presence was almost as disturbing as the sensations that had invaded her mind and touched her story.

He didn't seem inclined to talk either, driving slowly and carefully back to the house.

"You did very well tonight," he finally said as he let them inside the house. "I was impressed."

"Thank you, I think."

"Would you like something to eat, a snack?"

"What I'd really like is a drink. Do you have a beer?"

"Sorry, no beer. But I believe that Hattie kept a bottle of sherry. I could pour you a glass."

"No, never mind. If I can't tempt you into

joining me, I'd better not. I think I'll watch a little television and go to bed."

Nick smiled. Every time Dusty saw that wicked smile, she was surprised. It was so unexpected, and so perfect for the sardonic face it adorned.

"Fine, but maybe you'd better arm yourself with more than sherry. The only TV set in the house is in my bedroom. I'd enjoy the company, but the commercials always make me look for something to fill the time. You might not be safe."

This was what she'd wanted, but when she'd voiced her need, he'd refused. "No thanks. I'll pass." She pulled a book from Hattie's case, started up the stairs, then stopped. "I didn't hear the television set playing."

He turned out the lights and followed her up the stairs. "Ear phones. I didn't want to disturb Hattie."

Dusty moved ahead, down the corridor. "I never liked the things."

"Neither do I. But it puts the sound right in your mind. Keeps you from thinking or dreaming. I always thought thinking was the worst, but now I'm not so sure."

With that strange statement he stepped into his bedroom, gave her one last look of longing, and closed the door. He wished he had a cigarette, then realized that he hadn't smoked in days. Everything seemed to be changing.

Dusty, left in the darkened hallway, decided that reading might be fine for later. Now she needed action. She took a deep breath, moved down the corridor, found the light switch inside her room, and flipped it on. She decided that if she hurried, she could claim the shower first.

Moments later she was standing beneath the lukewarm spray of water, allowing it to cool her skin. Because she didn't have a dryer, she'd pinned her hair beneath a shower cap. Once she was clean—and calm—she dried herself, then realized that she was standing in the bathroom without a robe.

"No problem, Dusty, you have your night-shirt."

She hung the wet towel back on the rack and pulled the Florida Marlins T-shirt over her head. Tiptoeing to the door, she cracked it a hair and listened. Everything seemed quiet. Taking a deep breath, she opened the door and stepped into the hall. Nick was leaning against the frame of his open door.

"Marlins, huh? I'm a Saints fan myself."

There was a tightness in his voice that stopped her. "Are you spying on me?" she asked.

"Not unless I'm Superman. I don't see through walls too well."

"Magic men don't need to. They just dematerialize and, like a cloud of vapor, move through the wall."

"I'm no wizard, Dusty. I'm just a normal

flesh-and-blood man." Too normal, he thought, feeling his body surge to life at the sight of her with the light behind her.

"That's what I thought. It's you who keeps trying to claim that you're some kind of freak. I'm finished in the bathroom."

He moved down the corridor, stopping too close. In spite of her attraction to the man, he frightened her.

"So tell me," he said, his voice deepening. "What are we going to do about sharing this house?"

"Well, I've been thinking about that."

"And?"

The glow from a light in his room spilled out into the corridor. Her eyes were becoming adjusted to the half-darkness. He wasn't wearing a shirt and his jeans were unbuttoned, almost as if he'd been naked and just threaded his legs into them to step into the hall. A dark growth of whiskers on his face accented the hollows of his cheeks, drawing attention to eyes that continued to burn her skin with the intensity of his gaze.

"Why don't you sell me your half?" she asked.

He'd been stalling, only half listening, recovering ground already covered as he attempted to keep her from fleeing. But this proposition caught him by surprise.

Hell, almost everything she did surprised him.

"Where do you intend to get the money?"

"Old J.R. said I had plenty, remember?"

"I also remember that it was Hattie's wish that we share the house. The money was to be used to support the ART Station, wasn't it?"

"Not all of it. I asked. She left it to my discretion. I could make a down payment and pay you off in installments."

"Suppose I don't want to move?"

"Why wouldn't you? You're a doctor, a surgeon. You can help people. It would be wrong to hide here and not give what you can."

"What about you? It seems to me that a police officer gives. What's the difference?"

"The difference is that I can't be a law officer anymore. You can still be a doctor. Unless they've taken your license. They haven't, have they?"

"No. I still have a license. It's the knowledge I've lost."

"That doesn't make any sense."

He took a deep breath. "Believe me, Dusty. It's the truth. After the accident it was all gone. My medical knowledge vanished. I couldn't even take a temperature."

"Now I know you're pulling my leg. You treated the cut on my finger."

"An idiot could have done that."

"What about that woman in the restaurant?"

He hesitated. "That's a bit harder to explain. I didn't know what to do, until—" he might be baring his soul, but he couldn't bring himself to say that Dr. Sigmund Freud had suddenly appeared and showed him the procedure—"it suddenly came to me. Until then I didn't have a clue."

A strong breeze sprang up, whipping a tree limb against the roof of the porch, moaning around the corner of the house like the chorus in a Greek play.

The hall was cool and Dusty was still damp. Standing there, she began to shiver. "Knowledge? Or confidence?" she asked, her voice trembling. "I would, but I can't. You can, but you won't. Hattie knew what she was doing, didn't she?"

It must be the house, he thought, that seemed to feed his senses with fire. Until Dusty came, his life had been serene, pleasantly free from any complications. He'd transferred all his patients to his partner and removed his name from the door. After a few turndowns, they'd stopped any pretense of missing him. Only Bill, at the hospital, refused to let him simply exist. Bill and Hattie.

In her own way Dusty was as direct as Hattie. She couldn't understand his memory loss. Hell, he couldn't understand it himself, and he was a doctor. He'd alibied his efforts as being a result of ghostly intervention, uncertain whether his explanation was better or worse than the truth.

Until Bill had blindsided him in his office

with the X rays of the fetus with the tumor. He hadn't been able to forget about that, and the more he remembered, the easier it was. The hell of it was the uncertainty. Where he'd once been so confident that he would have attempted almost anything, now he held back.

"What's your problem, Merlin?" Dusty asked. "Out of magic dust?"

She wasn't going to let go. He'd managed to draw a line between himself and the rest of the world. Only Hattie and Bill had stepped over. Now Dusty. He was being forced to examine and defend his position. He didn't like that. And he didn't like the way she refused to let him be. He didn't even want to give voice to the need he felt to take her in his arms.

Trying to sort out his emotions was like trying to turn smoke into something solid. Smoke, sex, and surrender. The words became a kind of chant. Outside the house the wind blew again. There was a rainstorm coming.

There was another kind of storm already raging in the hallway. He could have waited in his room until she was finished. His motives for standing in the hall were selfish and primitive. He didn't have to prop himself against the wall and visualize droplets of water running over full breasts, circling around beaded nipples, finding a path through the soft hair between her legs, and making obscene ripples down long legs. But that was what was happening, and now all he wanted to do was plunge himself inside her and stop the twisting emotion that was messing up his mind and all his resolve.

A wise woman would have pushed her way past Nick and closed and locked the door behind her. But Dusty didn't know how to back down. Standing opposite her was like walking on a nylon carpet and coming in contact with something metal. Static electricity bounded off him, and they weren't even touching.

"So," she said in a voice that managed to be reasonably steady, "we've established that you're not Superman and I'm not Mary Poppins. You're not Merlin and I'm not Desirée. What does that make us?"

"Vulnerable," he said in a hoarse voice, and turned back into his room. "And ready to explode."

The storm broke in a fury, throwing lightning at the house and yard in a furious rage. Dusty lay in bed, shivering one minute and kicking off the covers the next. Nothing in her life up to now had prepared her for the rampaging emotions she felt every time she parted from Dr. Nick Elliott.

She turned on her stomach and punched her pillow into a lump. "I need to go to sleep. Hattie, if it's you and your spirit buddies who are causing this hullabaloo, I wish you'd stop. I'm hurting here."

Then, just as quickly as it had come, the storm moved away, leaving the house in some suspended state of calm. Dusty felt her nerve endings relax and her eyelids grow heavy, and finally she slept.

Dusty's dream began slowly, music playing softly. No, not music, a woman's voice humming. The woman was happy. She was bathing in some kind of hip bath, her hair pulled up on her head and her nightclothes draped across the foot of the bed.

Then she stood and began to dry herself, rubbing the towel across her breasts, down her stomach, and across the mound of light-colored hair between her legs. Her eyes were closed. The touch of the soft fabric against her body brought a shiver of anticipation. Dusty moved against the towel, feeling the flush of heat, the desire that was building.

Then she stepped from the tub and reached for the nightdress of delicate lace. She pulled it over her body, then released the mass of silver curls, allowing them to cascade down her back.

It was time.

He would come soon.

She lay down on the bed and waited, her lips curled into a smile.

Then, with no sound or warning, hands were touching her body, soft lips feathering her face and neck, warm breath heating her skin as his mouth moved lower to tease her breasts.

The woman didn't open her eyes. The room was enchanted. The woman was bewitched as her imaginary lover continued to caress her body, whispering indistinguishable words of love. She felt his body, strong and hard, against her. And she spread her legs, opening herself up to him, to that part of him that sought and found the core of her need.

Dream? Vision? Dusty wasn't sure. She only knew that her body was on fire. Her arms were clasping him tight against her, and she raised herself to meet his hungry thrusts with wild abandon. She wanted to wake up and let it be real. To take his mouth and ravish it. To run her fingers through his hair and know that the touch was real.

In the dream, across time, across the centuries, passion came rolling in, claiming and intensifying, turning the four-poster bed with its gauzy hangings into another world. Then that world exploded. There was such incredible joy and peace that it reverberated through Dusty's mind and rippled down her body into her soul.

Then she was abruptly awake, her body jerking with the aftermath of her vision, or her climax, or the enchantment under which she'd dreamed.

Her body was glowing. Her mind floating in some state of suspended animation. She couldn't think where she was, or what she'd feared. Only that he'd come to her in the night. The woman in the vision wasn't somebody from the past.

The woman was Dusty O'Brian.

As for the man, sorcerer, magician, apparition, whatever he was, or whatever she'd needed him to be, he'd made love to her in a way that she'd never thought possible.

And it had all been a dream.

Or had it?

The house was empty the next morning. Across the lawn were broken twigs and debris left over from the storm the night before. Dusty made coffee and buttered two pieces of toast as she tried to force her mind to sort out the half-memories of her dream.

Like a sleepwalker, she poured the coffee and ate the toast. Whatever she'd experienced the night before, she felt emotionally drained.

The phone had been ringing for several seconds before she heard it. "Hello?"

"Hello, is Nick there?" a strange voice asked.

"No. At least I don't think so. I haven't seen him this morning."

"You must be Dusty. I'm Bill Lewis, his friendly doctor and associate. Will you tell him that everything is looking good for the operation?"

Her heart stopped. "Nick needs an operation?"

The voice laughed. "No, not Nick. This is a procedure we're about to pioneer. Just tell him the team *would* like him to assist."

Dusty replaced the phone on its cradle. So, Dr. Nick Elliott was being invited to assist in a surgical procedure.

By lunchtime a messenger from Aunt Hattie's attorney had delivered a check which was by no means the small amount Dusty was expecting as walking-around money. She studied the cashier's check and decided she needed to open an account and do a little grocery shopping. It was time she checked out the village. Betty Hirt could advise her about banks and grocers.

It was David who was in the office. He motioned Dusty to come in as he carried on a telephone conversation. Absently she studied the scripts and brochures on the table by the door. There was a poster advertising the tour. *What does a Southern Ghost say? "Boo, Y'all"* was the catchy copyrighted phrase used on the playbill to promote the event.

She walked around the office while David was talking. On the wall were cast pictures, playbills announcing original works presented on the little theater stage, and newspaper reviews. One advertised an adaptation of a piece of popular fiction by a local author, Betty Hirt. Then she caught the gist of David's conversation.

"No, he isn't an artist, he's a doctor. Hattie talked Nick into accompanying our art teacher to the Children's Center at the hospital. He usually helps her load and unload the van and wanders around the activities room while she teaches. I've never heard of his using his medical skill before."

There was a silence. David was frowning and lifting his eyebrows to his unseen caller.

"I assure you, he is a licensed medical doctor, and if he thinks the child has a problem, I'd take him seriously."

A few more words and the conversation broke off. David sat for a moment, his mind on his conversation, before he remembered Dusty's presence. "Sorry, part of the job is putting out brush fires when they spring up. What can I do for you this morning?"

"I stopped to see if you'd recommend a bank. I have a check I'd like to deposit."

"Sure, one block over. Trust Company. Just ask for Joe Turner. He'll fix you up."

She thanked him, started to leave, then turned back. "Nick is with an art teacher?"

"Yes. We send an art teacher to the local grammar schools that don't have one. Two mornings a week our teacher goes to the children's hospital. When she's teaching the sick children, Nick goes along and drives our van. He's been a big help to Thelma."

"But there was a problem?"

"No, I don't think so, but I don't know yet. I'm sure it's nothing. By the way, we were very impressed with your performance last night. Have you decided on an ending yet?"

"No, but I'm working on it."

The phone rang again, and David turned back to it as Dusty left the building and began to walk along the sidewalk. Main Street was a picture postcard scene of quaint little shops, merchants sweeping the sidewalks, and motorists vying for one of the few parking spaces along the street. As she paused to look for the bank, she noticed a blue van embossed with brightly painted flowers.

A van being driven by Nick. He didn't see her. Which was just as well. It was at that moment that she knew beyond a doubt. The man in her dream the night before was no apparition. What happened might have been a dream within a dream.

She was the woman.

And the man who'd loved her was Nick Elliott.

The bank manager opened Dusty's account and issued her temporary checks. She didn't have enough money for a car. But she could buy a bicycle with a big enough basket to carry her groceries home. The hardware store owner attached double baskets to the rear of her machine and supplied her with a security lock.

At the grocery store she purchased three bags of food. Two went into the baskets, and one was tied around the handlebars. By the time she rode back into the yard, she felt as if she were back in charge of her life.

Nick didn't appear until late afternoon, sticking his head in the door and sniffing appreciatively. "I don't know what you're cooking, but if it tastes as good as it smells, I might have to marry you."

"It's good. I just tasted it."

He walked through the house and picked up the spoon. "May I?"

"You may. Then you have to call somebody named Bill. He says that the procedure has been approved, and you're going to help. I'm glad."

Nick swallowed the marinara sauce and put the spoon back on the counter. "He's wrong. I'm not going to help. I can't."

"Well, maybe I misunderstood, but I was sure that's what he said."

"No, you didn't misunderstand," Nick said, and turned to leave.

Dusty didn't like the sudden stiffness of his stance, nor the pallor that turned his face to chalk. Something was wrong. She searched her mind for a way to find out. "Nick, I saw you today, driving a blue van."

He paused. "Yes."

"David said you go with the art teacher. Why didn't you say something?"

"It's nothing. I only drive the van on the mornings when she visits the hospital. Some of the children are pretty sick. I can be of more help to the teacher in that kind of situation."

Even when he didn't have the confidence to treat them, Nick was drawn to children. Just as she had been when she'd tried to help the police officers' widows and their children.

"Did something happen today, something different?"

He turned and gave her a quick hard look. "What do you mean?"

"Well, I was in David's office when he got a call from someone, something about you examining a student."

"Damn! I knew that was mistake. But I couldn't let it go."

Dusty cut the temperature down to simmer and walked over to Nick. "Come along, Doctor, and tell me what happened."

He allowed her to lead him to the sofa, where he sat down and leaned back, closing those dark eyes and letting out an oath. "I should never have examined the boy. What if I'm wrong?"

"Wrong about what, Merlin? What's wrong with the kid?"

"Somebody has been using him as a punching bag. He was being very brave, trying to hide his bruises. It might not be obvious to others, but I knew."

"Of course you did, Nick."

"How can I be sure?"

"Any doctor would recognize those kinds of wounds. I'd recognize them. I sure saw enough."

"Dusty, I don't know whether it was the doctor in me who knew or just the human being."

She wanted to put her arms around him and comfort him, say that everything would be all right. But he wouldn't welcome that. She didn't even know how to let him know that she shared his uncertainty.

Finally she lifted his hand to her face and nestled her cheek in his palm. "I'm sorry, Nick. I wish I knew what to do to help."

His eyes flicked open and he looked at her with hunger. Not sexual this time, but the hunger of one person for another, of loneliness seeking a common bond to lighten the weight of the pain.

"You already have, Desirée. You're so much like Hattie. She wouldn't leave anything alone either. I'll bet you were a good cop."

"I was the best."

"And you should be again. Isn't there some way you can clear your name?"

"I don't know. Maybe. There's a man on the force who never believed that I was taking a bribe, but he couldn't prove it. He wanted me to stay, but I couldn't see any future in that."

"I remember," he said, "the tide coming in, surging around your ankles. When Hattie told you to come home."

She looked surprised. "I'd forgotten I told you that."

"It seems I'm not the only one who talks too much. What is there about us that makes us bare our souls to each other?"

She lowered his hand and laid it across her knees. "I don't know. I've never been one to talk about myself much. Nobody else ever seemed to care."

"I do. Tell me about the bribe."

And she told him, about learning that contributions to the charity were being skimmed off the top so that what was turned over to the Finance Allocations Committee was only a fraction of the money collected for widows and children.

"What did you do?"

"That's where I made my first mistake. I went to the director of the charity. Silly me, I thought it was some kind of mistake."

"And it wasn't?"

"No. Before I could get a handle on who the bad guys were, they were charging me with theft."

His fingertips were drawing little circles on her knee. "The last time I was in court, you were innocent until proven guilty."

"Oh, it didn't take long to find that. There was a large deposit made to my bank account.

Then a second one. A new car was delivered to my house, supposedly paid for in cash. And the director of the fund testified that I'd been the only one with access to the money."

"Were you?"

"Of course not. I never even saw the money. Only the envelopes from the contributors with the amounts noted on the outside. I entered them and kept the records."

"And the amount on the envelope wasn't the amount on the checks."

"No. There were two separate bank accounts. The real one, which I was responsible for administering, and the phony one where the real checks were deposited."

By the time she finished her revelation, their fingers were entwined and Nick's eyes were filled with compassion and understanding.

"You believe me?"

"Of course. Why would you lie about that? You've already served the time. Now you have to go back and find the real bad guys."

Dusty stood up abruptly. "No way am I ever going to set foot in the state of Florida again. I've put all that behind me, and that's where it's going to stay!"

"That's what I said too. And then I saw an X ray and a little boy who'd been abused. We can't turn our backs, Dusty. Life keeps catching us in a scissors hold and forcing us to face up."

"I'm going to stir the sauce," she said, backing out of the room. "We have to eat if we're going to practice."

"Good idea, Desirée. Have you figured out the ending?"

"No, but after another night of dreams like I had last night, my ghost story may be X-rated."

He sat up. "Dreams? If your dreams were anything like mine, I imagine we could increase the take from the tour by half again."

She stopped in the doorway and looked back at him, her eyes wide with shock. "You dreamed too? About what?"

"It started with the widow in your story, and a hip bath. I don't think I'd better tell you where it ended."

Dusty gasped.

"I think I already know."

EIGHT

Rehearsal that night drew a bigger audience as the other storytellers who hadn't heard Dusty finished their tales and joined Betty and David as they walked the tour.

This time Dusty didn't have to ask. Nick, once again, found his spot in the corner. She could see him, but the tour couldn't. As she had the first two times, she closed her eyes and tried to clear her mind, beginning to speak only when she felt the presence of the woman whose tale she was telling. Dusty began haltingly, then as the words came to her, she spoke more confidently.

"My name is Danielle. I live here, at Blessing House, the house my husband built for us before the war. My husband, Clay, was so proud when he rode away to fight for our way of life. But now he's missing. 'Wait for me,' he said."

Dusty turned toward her audience as if she were letting them in on the secret.

"They tell me he's dead, but I won't believe that. No, he would never leave me. I feel him here, in my heart." Dusty tilted her head. "But wait. He will be here. Listen. There, do you hear them? Hoofbeats? I hear them every night, but Clay never comes. Clay? Clay?"

Tonight Dusty's words were different. But the pain and the anguish were the same. She raised her eyes to the window, then dropped her head as before, tears rolling unbidden down her cheeks.

There was a sound, a movement from the crowd that distracted her for a moment, then, as if arranged, she moved her gaze back to Nick and felt the story take life again.

"Where are you, Clay? I can't see you. Speak to me. Tell me what to do."

As Dusty beseeched Nick with her eyes, she felt a veil of shadows fall between them. He was there, yet he wasn't. And the room fell away. She tilted her head, as though she were still listening. Another room began to take shape and form.

"Clay, are you here? Have you returned at last?"

In her mind the walls turned to windows. On one side there was a bed with a red satin spread. The smell of honeysuckle seemed caught in the air currents swirling about the room. The sound of drums, of cannon fire, or shots faded away, and then, turning to the door, she saw him standing there, her beloved.

As he reached out for her the grief-stricken woman took a step toward him, felt her arms pass straight through the vision of the soldier she'd waited for so long, and collapsed in a swoon.

There was a woman's cry, then silence.

"Dusty! Dusty! Are you all right?"

She seemed to float somewhere between consciousness and a dreamlike state that wrapped her in contentment. She didn't want to wake.

"Turn on some lights, Betty. Stand back so I can examine her!"

Dusty stirred. It was Merlin, no—Nick. He was taking her pulse, lifting her eyelids so that the sudden light blinded her. Then he gave her a sharp slap on the cheek.

The lingering veil of the past vanished and Dusty came fully awake. "Hell's bells, Merlin. If that's the kind of medicine you practiced, I'm not surprised you don't have any patients." She came to her feet, eyes snapping, rubbing her face. "Why'd you do that?"

"Why'd you scare the life out of me?" Nick's voice was angry as he tried to conceal the dreadful fear that had swept over him when she fell. He rose slowly as he studied her. "Is this your idea of an ending to the story?"

The low murmur of conversation around them reminded Dusty of where she was, and she turned to face the shock on both Betty's and David's faces.

"Yes!" Dusty answered with more authority than she felt. "What do you think?" she asked, doing some fast fabricating. "Will that scare the spooks?"

Betty gave David a confused look and took a step toward Dusty. "You mean this was all part of your story?"

"Sure. At least it was an idea I was trying out."

"I think," David said slowly, "that it might be a little too scary. Remember we have a lot of kids in the audience."

"Well, maybe I'll work on it a bit more," she said, and took a couple of unsteady steps. She came to a stop and looked back at Nick, who stepped up and took her arm.

"Let's get that costume back," he said, "before you do something to it. Then if you want to practice the story more, we'll do it at home."

With gratitude in her eyes, she allowed him to walk her to the costume room, where she quickly changed into her regular clothes. Then she headed for the car with Nick beside her.

Once inside, Nick started the engine and drove away from the park. Except this time he took a different drive and ended up at the edge of the lake. He stopped the car.

"Now, let's talk. What was that all about?"

"Sweet Jesus, I don't know," she said. "I just started telling the story and it was as if somebody else took over."

He thought about that for a minute. "Hattie?"

"Nope, this wasn't Hattie."

"Then who?"

She considered her answer carefully. She'd been called dishonest, overbearing, even a smart aleck, but she'd never been called crazy. "If I had to guess," she finally answered, "I'd say it was the woman in the story."

Nick took her hand, positioning his fingers on her pulse again. "Normal now. But back there it was very erratic. I don't like this, Dusty. When all this ghost business started, it was merely in fun. But you're being affected by it."

"I'm not the one seeing Sigmund Freud."

"No, you are having erotic dreams about ghosts."

That stopped her. She didn't know how to answer him, how to argue. He'd had the same dream, or something similar. Otherwise how would he have known about it? She glanced out of the car window. There was a full moon, reflecting itself in the water. It looked as if it were riding gently across the surface like a great mound of cream-colored butter set on its side. She noticed something else.

"What's that, Merlin, out there in the water?"

"That's the carillon. It plays music every morning, at noon, and at six in the evening."

The graceful stone building caught the light and sparkled like amber.

He went on. "There was some talk about removing it."

"By whom, the Jolly Green Giant? That thing looks pretty well settled in."

"State officials wanted to have part of the Summer Olympics out here, some boating event, but the carillon was in the way. In order to stage the event, they would have had to relocate the bell tower."

"But they aren't?"

"No, the committee moved the boating event."

"I'm glad," Dusty said. "I like things to be able to stay put once they've found their place in life."

"That would be nice," he said, deciding that she wasn't talking about structures at all. "But sometimes fate intervenes and forces us down another road."

"Isn't that the truth? Like you and your accident."

"And you and your little tour of the Florida state prison system."

Nick got out of the car and held out his hand, inviting Dusty to slide across the seat and join him. "I'm beginning to think that the important thing may be that we don't forget the road, in case we want to go home again."

Dusty felt her pulse rate increase the second she placed her hand in his, and followed him to a spot at the edge of the water. She wasn't sure whether he was talking about his accident, or finding his way back somewhere he wanted to be.

"Why don't you go home, Nick? You said you had a house. Do you still own it?"

"Yes. I do."

"If you didn't want to keep the connection to your former life, why didn't you sell it?"

He sat down on a bench beneath a large oak tree and pulled her down beside him. "I'm not quite sure. I never liked the house. I bought it because it was near one of my partners and my wife liked it. But I stayed at the hospital so many nights that my little room there seemed more like home."

"Tell me about your wife, Nick. What was she like?"

He sat for a long time, his thumb drawing little circles in her palm, as if he were constructing some kind of road map.

"She was nice. She loved me. She helped me become whatever the hell I was."

"Nice?"

"Yes. Lois was a nurse when I met her. She was a little older than me."

"She loved you and she helped you. That doesn't sound like a very exciting relationship, Merlin."

"Relationships don't have to be exciting to be successful, Dusty."

"Are you trying to convince me or yourself?"

Nick stood and, barely limping now, walked toward the edge of the waters. He didn't answer for a long time, and as Dusty's eyes grew more accustomed to the moonlit darkness, she could see the stiff back he kept toward her.

"Sorry, magic man, I didn't mean to pry. Your relationship with your wife was personal."

"You're right," he finally said. "I didn't love her. But she never stopped believing that I would. I didn't think it mattered."

Dusty didn't know what to say. All her troubles seemed insignificant in comparison. She only knew that if Nick had been hers, it would have mattered. She would have made it matter.

The very thought of being married to Nick, of having his arms around her every night, of sleeping with him—she felt liquid heat boil up inside and fall to a spot at the junction of her thighs where it settled and simmered.

Whoa, Dusty, this is not smart thinking. You have as much chance of being married to Merlin as you do of being a cop again.

Knowing that was pure imagination, Dusty forced herself to a safer line of thought. She hadn't meant to turn Nick back into the stone man, not when he was loosening up and coming close to being human. For the time being, they were still roommates, and she didn't feel like walking back from wherever they were.

"Nick," she said, and moved down to where he was standing. "I'm sorry. If what you shared with your wife made her happy, you mustn't keep blaming yourself if you didn't feel the same."

He turned back to her.

"But I was responsible, and the hell of it is that if the accident hadn't happened, I would have gone on hurting her and she'd have let me."

"Yep. That sounds like love," Dusty said, placing her hands on his shoulders. "Men always hurt the women who love them, and the women always let them."

"But I never loved her, Dusty. That's what's killing me."

"Did she know that for sure?"

"I never told her. She thought I was so dedicated to saving lives that I was a poor husband. Then one day, when I was well established, I'd have time for her. I wouldn't have."

"She never knew, Nick. Trust me. Women always create the life they want in their minds. If it isn't really like that, they just wait until it is. We're stubborn that way."

"Then you're fools," he snapped.

"That too," Dusty agreed. "Now, take me home, Merlin. I need my sleep if I'm going to create a fantasy tomorrow night when the real tour begins."

"Would you like to see my house?" he asked unexpectedly.

She was surprised. "Ah, sure. I'd like to see it. If you want me to."

"We'll go in the morning, if that suits you."

They returned to the car. But the mood was somber. The air seemed hot and heavy, and the stillness was overwhelming. Nick was struggling to understand how he came to confide in Dusty. Even more, he wondered how in hell he came to invite her to go to his house. The yard man cut the grass and the cleaning woman came by every week and dusted, but Nick never went back. He'd thought that he'd closed off the past. Now he was opening it up again.

Dusty felt as if she'd been cut into fragments. There was the storyteller who had been coerced into taking Hattie's place in a life that was drawing her in deeper and deeper. Then there was the little girl who was ready to reclaim her spot in the tree house. And finally there was the new woman carrying the seeds of the passion that Nick had planted deep inside her. She felt like one of those bulbs whose growth the nurserymen accelerated until it burst into bloom in the wrong season. She was changing, and the lines between the past and the future were blurring.

By the time they reached the house, neither was capable of general conversation. Yet that was all they could allow, all they trusted from themselves.

"Would you like coffee?" Dusty asked.

"No coffee. I need to sleep at some point."

"Coffee keeps you awake?" she whispered.

"No. I mean I don't sleep soundly. I haven't since Hattie died."

She couldn't help asking, "Is it me? Am I interfering with your rest?"

"Hell yes, but you could be kind and let me blame it on the coffee."

"I'm sorry," she managed to choke out. "I'll go to bed and leave you alone."

"Lock the door, Dusty."

"Why, am I in danger?"

He swore. "One of us is."

She thought of something and stopped halfway up the steps. "You remember that dog I told you to get? You thought I was kidding."

Nick's laugh was sardonic. In the hallway below, she could see the scar on his face, as if it were giving confirmation of his warning. He seemed even leaner, more predatory.

"With my luck, wildcat, any dog I bought would be a werewolf in its other life, and I'd have to lock us both up every time there was a full moon."

Nick might have slept that night, but Dusty didn't. She twisted and turned until watery smears of light splattered across the fading night sky.

"It won't work, child," she could hear Hattie's voice saying. "You can't wish the bad things away. You have to cover them up with stardust."

She'd told Dusty that after her mother had died. And together they'd built an imaginary boat in which they'd placed her mother's spirit. Then in a solemn ceremony in the backyard, they'd released the boat into the night sky, holding hands and chanting as they imagined its climb.

"Now she's free," Hattie had said. "And she's where she will never feel pain again, unless you cause it."

"Me?" Dusty had asked.

"Of course. She'll always be up there in the heavens, with the angels. But she can see you. If you need her, she's there."

Their conversation came back to Dusty in the darkness as clearly as if it had happened the day before. And then she understood what she had to do. Hattie was still here, waiting. It was so simple. It explained why Dusty had been sent back. Why Nick was there.

Hattie needed to be set free, to fly with the angels.

When the time was right, she'd explain it to Nick.

Dusty closed her eyes and slept.

Across the hall Nick let out a long, troubled

breath. Suddenly the house was peaceful, his jangled nerves seemed to smooth out and his eyelids grew heavy.

In the morning he'd take Dusty to see his house. Once she saw, she'd understand why he had left. Then they'd talk about Hattie's house and decide what to do.

Tomorrow Dusty would tell her story before the first tour. She'd do well. She'd shown that when she'd pretended to faint. Or had she? Her pulse had been jumping all over the scale, though it could have been from excitement. Still, the scene had been realistic—too realistic. He was worried about the woman who had come to stand for desire in his life. There was not a second of his day that she wasn't in his thoughts.

Soon, he'd have to make a decision about assisting Bill in the surgery.

Soon, he'd have to decide what in hell he was going to do about the wildcat that Hattie had somehow conjured up to bewitch him and break down the safe walls behind which he'd hidden himself.

"Ah, Hattie, you're the sorcerer, not me. You've cast a magic spell over this house, and I don't know how to break it."

Downstairs the curly orange and black ribbon on the outside of the doorknob slipped to the floor. A quick, teasing wind swept across the front porch and carried the ribbon away, dipping and swaying, until finally it disappeared in the night sky.

The night watchman patrolling the grounds of the plantation glanced up and saw the curly shadow moving across the sky.

"Spooks!" he said in unease. "They always stir things up when they start telling them stories out here. There's some things folks just ought not to mess with."

"Tom Glavin, the Atlanta Braves pitcher, lives in this house," Nick said as they drove down the street. "He's a golfer, pretty good."

"And I guess there's a golf course?"

"Sure. That's one of the measures of success, golf courses and tennis courts. Of course, each house has its own pool."

"You have a pool?" Dusty couldn't keep the awe from her voice.

"Of course. And a sauna and an exercise room. At least those rooms got used. The rest of the house seemed pretty empty."

So much for her surmising that he had used all his money to pay his hospital bills. As they drove into the garage and the automatic doors closed behind them, Dusty felt like the fool she'd said women often were.

This was wealth such as she'd never experienced before. To someone like her, it would be like finding the genie in the magic lamp who granted three wishes. Dusty probably would have started with wealth as her first wish. A real lover would be the second. The third? That was harder, children perhaps. If Dusty owned the genie, she'd hold on to that last wish.

The house wasn't empty of furniture. It was decorated beautifully in shades of sand and burgundy with touches of blue to accent. Nick showed her the gleaming white kitchen, the low couches in the living room, the pickled oak furniture in the dining room, and, finally, the master bedroom.

Dusty let out a deep sigh. "Wow! I'm impressed." She wandered around the room, lifting the silver-framed pictures that had been arranged on the dressing table, across the built-in bookshelves, and on the night table. The woman smiling at her was short and blond, older than Dusty had expected. The expressions of the people told the truth.

In the wedding picture the woman's smile seemed hesitant but warm. A snapshot on the golf course where she and Nick were seated with another couple, caught her as she was looking at Nick. Her expression was less confident. And finally, the last picture was of a woman who knew pain and lived with it.

"Lois?" she asked, holding up the group picture.

"Yes. That was Lois. The other man is my partner, and that's his wife."

"Lois looks as if she isn't very comfortable with them. It would be hard to live the life of the rich and famous if you didn't fit in. I could relate to that."

Nick walked to the window and opened the drapes. "It wasn't Lois who didn't fit in, Dusty. It was me. All this was her world, her life, her money. When we got married, I didn't even have tuition money for the next quarter. She paid for it—and me."

"Is that what you brought me here for, to show me that you don't deserve this? Well, I don't buy that, Nick. I believe that when you get married, what's mine is yours and what's yours is mine. I'd never sign any premarital agreement, and I'd never marry anybody unless I planned to love him forever, no matter what. And I'll bet that Lois felt the same way."

"But she's the one who died. All this is mine now. And I feel like a thief."

Dusty was becoming angry and she wasn't quite sure why, unless it was because they were discussing a woman in her own bedroom, as if she couldn't hear. It was uncomfortable and Dusty couldn't stop herself from whirling around and dashing down the stairs. She unlocked the glass doors leading out onto a patio overlooking the pool.

For a long time she stood and stared at the water. The occasional breeze that swept around the house ruffled the water and made little waves that slapped the tiled sides of the pool.

The last time she'd looked down at waves, she'd been ready to kill herself. But Hattie hadn't let her. Somehow, from someplace deep in her mind, she'd heard Hattie urging her to come home. And she'd stepped back from the brink.

"It's too bad that it isn't warmer," Nick's voice said from behind her. "We could go for a swim."

"Why? So you could wallow in recriminations again? Well, I don't buy that, Nick Elliott. You and Lois lived here. This was your house. If you don't feel comfortable with it, sell it. The only way you'll get the hurt out of here is to fill it with stardust."

"I don't know what you mean," he answered. "I know you call me Merlin and I know you think that something magical is happening, but there's no stardust here. It's just smoke. The truth is, there is an overpowering sexual attraction between us, and that's playing havoc with our psyches."

"You don't believe in stardust, Merlin? Fine. Let's go. I've seen enough of your shrine to guilt."

Nick followed her around the house and to the car. "Aw, come on, Dusty, you don't believe in all this magic stuff. Only a few days ago you were ready to go to bed with me. I didn't read that wrong, did I?"

"No," she admitted. "You didn't read that wrong. I'm very attracted to you."

"And that didn't have anything to do with wealth or lifestyles, did it? It was simply a man and a woman who wanted each other."

She walked around the pool and into a flower garden riotous with bronze and yellow mums. She leaned down and picked one. But there was no sweet scent. The flowers were like the house, beautiful but cold. She was delaying responding to Nick's suggestion.

He was wrong, and this was the wrong place to be. Or maybe it wasn't. Maybe it would be easier to talk here, where Lois's touch acted as a governor on her emotions.

"You're wrong, Nick, about wealth and life-styles. I could never feel comfortable in a place like this. It's too perfect. And I'm not. I have too many warts to be a princess. But you could be a prince."

"I never wanted to be a prince. I just wanted to be a doctor. And I used Lois to become one."

"Yes, you did. Now you're a doctor. Why aren't you practicing?"

His eyes darkened in the sunlight, taking on the harnessed fury of some caged wild animal. "I have my reasons."

She gave a dry laugh.

"You know what's so funny, Nick? I actually

thought you might be poor. I thought I'd buy your half of the house so you'd have the money to get your life back together. Can you believe that? I was ready to give you money, the way Lois did. But you didn't need my money, did you? You were turning down my help. Why?"

"Because I'm a damned fool, I suppose."

"No, I think it's because you're still punishing yourself. Too bad. Maybe we'd both be better off if we'd made love and gotten past that hang-up. Having a conscience is hell!"

"Thank you, Dr. Freud," he said. "At least I'm seeing things clearly. You keep trying to pretend that your past is dead. You're trying to cover up the attraction between us with magic as if giving lust a spiritual connotation makes everything different. You're just blowing smoke. I still refuse to believe in magic."

"You do? Well, stick with me, Merlin. Sooner or later, I'm going to have to change your mind. I'm going to show you magic smoke and stardust too."

NINE

Dusty had never been more nervous in her life. Facing the judge for sentencing hadn't been as trying. She'd already been pronounced guilty at that point and nothing could be worse.

Until now.

Standing in the dressing room, she applied light makeup and looked at her face in the mirror. Tonight she had to face the tour with a story that was still unfinished. She'd promised Betty that she'd use one of the two endings that had been provided. But she hadn't a clue which way she'd go. Not only that, but the woman looking back at her in the mirror seemed just as vague and distraught.

All around Dusty were the other storytellers, wearing various kinds of period costumes appropriate to their story. She could see the crusty old sea captain, wearing his cap, the elegant older man wearing a black frock coat and wrinkled trousers, and the woman wearing a maroon cape that tied beneath the neck.

Each of them had been issued a lantern which would be lit and used for movement through the dark grounds and as a prop at their site.

Nick had left her at the dressing room and disappeared to check on the gazebo where a post had been reported to be unsteady. They were allowed to use the plantation in exchange for providing the art classes to the schools and the Children's Center at the hospital, but Nick was responsible for making certain that no damage was done.

In the mirror, Dusty saw Betty bounce into the room. "Hey, Dusty, look what I found. A frog for your hair."

She came toward Dusty, holding out a crocheted hair net.

"Isn't this great? It's just like the picture."

Dusty felt a shiver race down her spine. "Where'd you find that?"

"Some woman brought it by the Station. Said we might like to add it to our costume wardrobe. Sit down and let me put it on your hair."

Dusty laughed. "Sit down? In this hoop?"

"Here." Betty pulled a stool over to the mirror and lifted Dusty's hoop. "Sit!"

She complied, glad to be off her feet for a few

minutes. Silently she watched as Betty fitted the net over her hair and pinned it in place. "Now all you have to do is add the pin, and you're a dead ringer for the woman in the painting."

"Add what pin?"

"The broach. I gave it to the wardrobe mistress this morning."

Dusty's throat grew tight. "Did some mysterious woman suddenly appear with that too?"

"No, the plantation curator had it all along. Whoever donated the painting also donated the broach. We're just being allowed to borrow it for this tour. Do be careful. If anything happens to it, they'll string me up in a heartbeat."

With the addition of the broach, the picture was complete. Even Betty was taken aback by Dusty all decked out in a costume that had suddenly come together with the unexpected addition of the jewelry.

"Well, I'm off," Betty said. "I have to check out the tour guides." She started toward the door, then turned back to Dusty. "Don't worry," she said, giving Dusty a quick hug, "this will be a piece of cake. You're truly special. I knew it that first night when you were on the stage at the Station."

Dusty could only nod. She wasn't certain about Betty's conviction, though she did feel different. In the mirror she could almost see an aura around her, not red as Nick had said, but a silver color.

She shivered again, then took her lantern and, with the other storytellers, made her way toward her spot. As she entered the back door she followed the path the tour would take, up the steps, into the main corridor, and down the foyer to the parlor. There was a hush, almost as if the house were waiting.

Standing beneath the portrait, Dusty looked up at the woman, making an instant connection with her eyes—silver-gray eyes that penetrated, that asked, that demanded something from Dusty in return.

"All right, Aunt Hattie," she whispered. "I feel your hand in all this. I don't know how you did it, but it's done. I'm standing here, wearing a dress that mysteriously appears, a net that is presented anonymously, and a broach that seems to have been here all along. What next?"

But there was no answer. Only the penetrating glare of the woman who seemed to be watching.

"So, Hattie isn't involved," Dusty went on, looking up at the picture. "So it's you. Who are you, and what is it you want me to do?"

Again there was no answer.

Something was out of kilter. She'd felt it before. There was something pulling her to the hallway. She even took several steps away from the doorway and glanced around.

Through the windows she could see the line of people at the gate. They were buying tickets and being divided into groups. The first tour started down the walk. That meant she still had some fifteen minutes before they would get to the house.

Across the foyer was the formal dining room, set for tea instead of a meal. She stood at the rope and studied the room. The strange feeling that the house was waiting intensified. There was almost a vibration in the air, a sense of expectation humming beneath her feet.

"Nerves!" she said, and turned back to the parlor, allowing her gaze to fall on the stairs.

Up there.

Dusty whirled around. "Who said that? Is there someone here?"

There was no answer. She had an incredible urge to climb the stairs. She wanted to go up. She needed to go up. But her feet refused to move.

That's where Nick found her, standing at the foot of the narrow stairway, looking up as if someone were standing at the top talking to her.

"Dusty? Dusty! Are you all right?"

When she turned to face him, he was stunned at the pallor of her face, at the struggle in her eyes as she tried to focus on him, finally bringing the light of recognition back, recognition and life.

"Nick," she whispered, and came to him, laying her face against his chest. "It's you."

He felt her heart beating, the trembling of

her arms as she pressed herself against him. "I thought someone was up there, someone calling to me."

"There's no one up there. Only two large rooms, totally empty."

"Are you sure there's nothing else?"

"Only the door at the top of the steps, but it's padlocked and the lock is so rusty that you couldn't get in there even if you wanted to."

"I don't know what's wrong with me."

"You're just under a lot of pressure. If you don't feel up to telling Hattie's story, we'll skip this spot and keep the tour moving. You tried, that ought to be enough to meet the requirements of Hattie's will."

Nick's arms tightened around her protectively. He'd never known such a surge of tenderness. She was afraid and she'd turned to him. All he wanted to do was hold her, to make things safe for her.

Gradually she relaxed, finally letting out a long, deep sigh. "Thank you, Merlin," she whispered. "I told you all along you have magic hands, hands that heal. I feel as if I've been asleep."

She even yawned, curling against him like a contented cat, burrowing in a warm spot of sunlight. She was rubbing his back, allowing her hands to slide lower, capturing his buttocks in her fingertips.

"Do you feel sleepy, Nick, as if you're dreaming?"

"Ah, no. In fact, if you don't stop that little body excursion you're making, you're going to find out what kind of dreams I have when I'm wide awake."

"Wouldn't you like to take me up those stairs and ravish me, the way Clark Gable ravished Vivien Leigh in *Gone With the Wind*?"

"Take a look at those stairs, Dusty. I'm not even sure your hoops will make it up. As for the ravishing, I thought we'd already decided that was a no-go."

"Maybe we were wrong."

A minor tremor raked his body at the thought of what she was suggesting. At the sudden strong urge he felt to comply, he almost took a step toward the stairs, then, blinking his eyes against the sudden flare of lantern light from beyond the front windows, he turned Dusty toward the parlor and into the corner that was always hidden in shadows.

"Dusty, darling, are you sure you're all right? You haven't been dipping into the widow's bottle of peach brandy to get into the mood, have you?"

"Is there brandy? Fine, let's have a toast." Dusty heard her voice, recognized the slightly slurred speech patterns she'd suddenly adopted, then flung her head back and smiled wickedly. "What's the matter, Clay, don't you want me?"

"If you don't stop that," he managed to say as her lips grazed his chin and nibbled on his earlobe, "we're going to be caught behaving in a very naughty manner by the tour group."

"Kiss me," she said breathlessly, "then I'll behave."

He wanted to. The group wasn't there yet. But this was no time to begin something that up to now, both had instigated, then stopped. This time he was having trouble. Heat was pooling in his loins and sizzling his thought processes. This time she was totally willing, enticing, hot. They were heading toward an explosion on the same time schedule. Neither pulled back. Neither was saying no.

Then the back door opened. Footsteps and laughter moved toward them. Nick came back to the present with a crash.

"Dusty!" He shook her. "Dusty, the tour is almost here. You have to tell your story. Dusty!"

Almost like a sleepwalker coming slowly awake, she turned sleepy eyes on him, allowed her arms to fall back to her sides. Moments later she smiled, turned away, and took her place beneath the portrait.

Nick stepped back into the shadows, wishing his heart would stop pounding, wishing the hair on the back of his neck would lie down and that whatever the hell kind of whirlwind they'd stirred up would calm itself.

The tour group seemed to sense instantly

that something was different. Their chatter hushed. Dusty cast her eyes on them, seeing yet not seeing.

She assumed the posture of the widow and started the story again, just as before, by closing her eyes and telling the listeners to empty their minds. She set the scene, describing her plantation, her husband, and their great love. Then came the war and he'd ridden away. The servants had vanished, one by one.

Now she was alone. They said Clay was dead, but she didn't believe them. She had promised to wait forever and she would.

"Eternity is a long time. But I have to stay, to wait. I promised."

She had them. Nobody was moving. No children tugging impatiently at the parent's hands. No loss of interest that instigated muted conversations among the group. Every eye was glued on Dusty or the portrait under which she stood.

As she talked Dusty seemed to grow paler, more frail, older, even. Behind her, if anybody besides Nick had noticed, the portrait seemed to come alive. From the first, he'd noticed the resemblance between the woman and Dusty, and now that resemblance intensified.

"Listen. Do you hear it? Hoofbeats. Clay, are you there?" Dusty ran to the window, then turned back to the doorway, as if she were hearing the horse ride around the house. Her gaze directed somewhere beyond the listeners, she watched without speaking.

Then, as before, she let out a joyous cry, then collapsed on the floor. As if on cue, the lantern went out and the room went dark. Nick rushed toward Dusty, his figure caught in the light through the windows like a silhouette.

Someone screamed.

"My goodness," another cried out. "I believe it really is a ghost."

"Now let us move on," the tour guide said hurriedly. "Through the front door to the lawn, where our last storyteller is waiting."

She managed to herd the group away from the parlor and outside. Nick, holding Dusty in his arms, felt her agitation, then suddenly her lips parted and her breathing came light and fast. She began to moan, not in pain, but in something like ecstasy.

He continued to hold her, almost afraid to wake her, completely mesmerized by the vision she made in the light spraying through the window.

Then he felt her body began to undulate. Pressing herself against him, she was asking, and some imaginary lover was responding.

But it wasn't him.

Moments later she shuddered, then went limp in his arms. The smile on her face was one of total satisfaction.

Nick Elliott was as aroused as he'd ever been

in his life, and the woman who'd caused this state of anxiety was floating in what appeared to be sleepy afterglow in his arms.

What in hell was happening?

The answer that came to him surfaced from the depths of his mind. *Don't ask questions, Nicky, just go with the flow. But don't wait too long. I don't think there's much time.*

He took her home and put her to bed. She talked to him, yet he was never certain that she was totally awake.

"Stress," he told himself.

"Spirits," she contradicted sleepily.

"It's just the mind's way of handling a situation that you don't want to face," he said, repeating the words he'd been told when he realized that he'd lost part of his memory. Then he realized that not only was she not listening, she was sleeping soundly.

Off came the costume. She couldn't sleep in a hoop. The undergarments seemed uncomfortably authentic, and he removed them as well, revealing her firm breasts with full pink nipples. The scrap of lace that covered her lower body was almost nonexistent. Nothing at all like what the real widow would have worn.

It was then that he saw it, the tattoo that he'd spoken of in such cavalier terms on her arrival. It was on her thigh, etched in blue and silver: a sliver of a moon from which was hanging a star. Trailing beneath the design was a delicate suggestion of . . . stardust.

He felt himself harden once more. In fact, he was never totally free of the incredible sexual urge that flared between them. Her spell had merely intensified as she wove her ghostly tale in the darkness of the plantation parlor. He still couldn't begin to understand where she went when she began to speak or how much she was experiencing and how much she was simply creating. But it was obvious to him that sexual climax had been the end result.

At least for her.

He was reduced to touching her, to feeling that breast and seeing the nipple pucker beneath his touch.

She moaned.

He groaned and started to move away.

"Don't go, Clay," she whispered. "I've waited so long—so long. Stay with me."

"No," he said with a groan. "I can't. *I* want you—Nick—not Clay. I can't take advantage of you if you don't know the difference."

She let out a dramatic sigh. "I know. Kiss me, my magic man."

At that point he knew she was awake, awake and tempting him. He struggled with this idea, wondering why they continued to tempt each other, push and then pull away. As she reached up and pulled him down, he lost the battle and brushed his lips across her parted ones.

"You know what you're asking for, wildcat?"

"Oh, yes," she said, wildness surging through her veins. "Oh, Nick."

"Why? Why me? Why now?" But his question got lost in the heat of her touch, in the willingness of her body to mold itself to him, in the incredible pounding of two heartbeats that rumbled like a freight train skidding down a mountain incline and its echo.

And then he was kissing her and kissing her, over and over, tasting, touching, seeking. In the moonlight she could see the lean, hard planes of his face, the scar, the incredible strength and power of the man. His eyes were closed, as if he wanted nothing to interfere with the hot sweeping caresses he was making.

He pulled away briefly, then as she rose to follow him, he pushed her back. "I can't stop," he rasped out. "God knows, I tried. But the need is always there and it's growing stronger. I can't think about anything but plunging myself inside you. And tonight I will."

Then he was sprawled across her, his hard pulsating manhood caught between them. She spread her legs, opening herself to him, moaning in soft urgency. But he didn't respond. Instead his fingers slipped down her body, seeking that place that throbbed in hot desire beneath the lace.

In her most secret place she felt a flood of heat rising beneath his touch. Nothing had prepared her for these feelings. No place she'd ever been, nobody she'd ever known had forged such intimacy, such need.

She gave a soft cry and put her arms around his neck, forcing him closer. But he refused to move completely over her. Everything felt so right. Her softness against his hardness, her body seeking and finding the heat that he was emitting. This was meant to be. There was no doubt in her mind now as every fiber of her being asked and reached out for this man.

Her fingertips found scars that rippled beneath her touch, her lips found corded neck muscles. Then, as he continued to drive her mad with his hands, she slid her hand down between them, searching for that part of him he was withholding. But he was maddeningly out of reach, and she was bordering on exploding.

"Nick! Please, Nick. Open your eyes. Look at me! I need to know that this is as real for you as it is for me."

His hands stilled.

His eyes opened.

And then she knew. He was as totally committed as she.

"I always knew," she whispered, "that this was an enchanted place. It was too important. I needed it too much. And it's called me back every day that I've been away. I just didn't know why."

"You still don't," he said with a growl. "This is lust, lady—pure, raw, unadulterated sex—and it's damned good. Don't make it more than it is."

He moved over her and found her aching secret place, then drove himself inside. Her body closed around him and she cried out at the exquisite wonder of his invasion.

As he moved she felt the swell of heat increase, the quick hot response that met his passion and caught fire. She'd known instinctively that it would be like this with Nick. Now they were moving together like that sleek, powerful train in the night, building and building until at last they flew over the edge and found what they'd both fought against, longed for, and feared.

Completion.

Peace.

Afterward she clung to him, her skin moist with sweat. He lay still, as if he were as stunned as she. Then he eased off her and collapsed beside her, his breathing coming deep and fast.

She turned her head and studied him in the faint light coming from the hallway. She touched his face, instantly aware of the return of his tension.

"Don't touch me." His voice was ragged and hoarse.

She continued her light caress. "A little late for modesty, isn't it, Merlin? Besides, I like touching you."

"You're a strange woman, Dusty O'Brian. I'll bet you brought home all the strays to care for."

"Except for this place," she said carefully, "I never had a home. But yes, I looked after those who needed me."

"Like who?"

"There was a woman once. Her name was Martha. She lived on the streets. I brought her food every day for a year, took her to the doctor, looked out for her. Then one day I saw her driving by in a limo."

"I don't understand."

"Her family found her and took her home. She never even said good-bye. I didn't hear from her again."

In a surprising move, his arm slipped around her, drawing her head against his chest. "Not like Hattie, huh?"

"No, not like Hattie."

They lay quietly for a time. Dusty was afraid to speak, afraid to break the fragile mood of belonging that seemed to have fallen over them.

Finally he started to move away.

"What are you doing?" she asked.

"I'm . . . I don't know. We shouldn't have done this, Dusty," he answered, and sat up on the side of the bed.

"Why? You'll never convince me that you weren't as involved as me."

"I wouldn't even try. At one time I thought we'd sleep together and that would get rid of that old sex thing that keeps getting in the way of a resolution to our problem."

"And it didn't?"

"No. I'm afraid it made things worse. We can't share a bed, Dusty. We can't even share this house."

She felt a sharp pain stab her in her chest. He meant it. They'd made the most incredible love she'd ever experienced, and he was saying that it had been a mistake. She couldn't let him be the one to walk away. She had to do something—fast.

"Well, I only have one thing to say, magic man. You have another life, another house. This is the only one I have. If you truly don't want to be with me, then go."

He stood and looked down at her. Her face was flushed, her silver hair spread across the pillow. She was the most enchanting woman he'd ever met. In spite of her prickly outer shell, she was warm and giving. What in hell was he going to do now that she'd put it on the line?

He shuddered. "I can't, Dusty. And yet I know I ought not to be here in your bed. It's not fair to you."

She raised herself up, unaware of the picture

she made lying there in the bed still filled with the smell of their lovemaking.

"You don't have to worry about that. I'm already a fallen woman. I was destroyed before I got back here. You can't do much more to me than has already been done."

"Nobody stays down if they want to get up, Dusty. Maybe it's time you thought about going back to clear your name."

"I can't. I'm not sure I want to go through the pain again."

"But there are some things that are worth the risk."

"You mean like going back to the operating room, Doc? I think the problem is that the part of us that's here is safe and secure. The part that ought to leave isn't nearly as tough as we'd like it to be."

She was too close to the truth. How in hell could he talk her into doing something that he couldn't?

"Philosophy?" he said, his voice sharp with recriminations. "Is that how you finish off a good roll in the hay, wildcat?"

His question was intentionally cruel, bringing the lovemaking back to what it had to be, pure hot sex, nothing more. He didn't want her to force him to face issues, to answer questions, to doubt.

And he knew that no matter how rough he was, the reason he couldn't go had nothing to do with medicine. It was because he didn't want to leave her.

"I'm flexible, Merlin. And I'm cold. Stop beating yourself up. Come back to bed with me. What's done is done. We can't go back and we can't change it. Why not enjoy whatever it is that we can give to each other for as long as it lasts?"

He looked at her for a long time. Then he forced himself to leave. He'd used Lois, he couldn't do that again.

"Coward!"

He closed his ears to the soft sound of her laughter as he closed the door.

"Hattie," he said with a growl, "if you're doing this, you've got to stop. I can't deal with her and all the rest. All I wanted to do was put the past behind me. She's making it fall all over me. You started it, you've got to stop it."

"I can't, Nicky." Hattie's voice answered as clearly as if she were standing beside him. He almost reached out to touch her, so sure was he that she was there. "You're on your own. I can't change what is going to happen."

"Why?"

"It really is up to you," she whispered. "It always has been. I'm only allowed to help. That's why I brought Siggy back. Though," she said with a chuckle, "at this stage of the game, maybe I ought to look up Rudolph Valentino. She's right, Nicky, what you need, you already have."

Nick rubbed his arms and shivered and paced back and forth down the corridor.

"What's wrong now?" Hattie asked.

"Aside from every other interfering you've done, I'm cold."

"Well, it is a bit cool for nudity."

Nick glanced down at his bare body. "Damn!" He strode down the corridor to his room. "You're a Peeping Tom, Hattie. Though I suppose that's the nature of ghosts. Not that I believe in ghosts. Are you going to be here from now on? Is this house going to remain haunted?"

"No. I'm only here as long as I'm needed. Once you send me away, I'll be gone."

"That can't be too soon for me," Nick said, pulling on a pair of briefs. "First I've got an angel tempting me twenty-four hours a day. And now there's a nosy spirit following me around. I ought to move back home and leave both of you. What do you think of that, Hattie Lanier?"

But there was no answer.

He was alone, and being alone now was different. He knew what he could have had, a woman in his arms who was willing and a friend who refused to let him fool himself anymore.

For one wistful moment he wished he were a wizard. A magic spell might be the only answer to the dilemma he was facing.

TEN

The next morning Nick decided that Dusty's ghost box was living quarters for an entire colony of spirits. There was no other logical explanation.

Logic? For a no-nonsense man, he was turning as squirrelly as Hattie and Dusty.

Dusty. He had spent the early hours of the morning trying not to think about Dusty, about what had happened between them, about how he'd feel if he'd woken and found her body entwined with his. Instead, he'd forced himself to concentrate on convincing himself that Hattie's voice was a figment of his imagination, an unexplained phenomenon associated with his accident, another weird memory quirk.

In the end, Nick was ready to concede that, imagined or otherwise, if Hattie had managed to call up Sigmund Freud in some kind of misguided attempt to help Nick regain his memory, her efforts were paying off. For in his effort not to think about Dusty, he seemed to free his mind, and like water pouring down a mountain in a snow melt, his medical knowledge came pouring back.

The process was overwhelming.

As a doctor, Nick had heard his professors and associates talk about a higher power, about miracles that came from some place beyond their expertise, but he'd never consciously experienced it. If a patient unexpectedly recovered, or if something happened he couldn't explain, he'd simply accepted it and taken the credit.

He didn't understand spiritual things, but something remarkable was happening, something that defied explanation. The question was, if he could see a man in a dark suit with gray whiskers named Siggy, why couldn't he see Hattie, in whose presence he was much more ready to believe?

Somehow she'd managed to bring him and Dusty together. Hattie had set the stage, but it had been they, Dr. Nicholas Elliott and Ms. Desirée O'Brian, who'd made the final connection. He'd tried to stop what he now recognized as the inevitable. But in the end, he'd made love to Dusty, linking them, forging a bond that even now tugged at him with such force that it was all he could do to sit at the kitchen table and try to analyze his desire.

The telephone rang. It was Bill Lewis pleading with Nick to come down to the hospital and sit in on the planning session for the surgery they were going to attempt on the fetus.

"I'm not ready," Nick argued. "I won't do it."

That's when the trouble began. The top shot off the coffeepot and the lights started switching themselves off and on. Finally, in self-defense, he recanted his refusal. "All right. I'll come in the morning, just to observe, Bill. Nothing more."

The kitchen arsenal grew quiet.

"Thanks, Nick. I'm glad to hear it. This baby needs a miracle to live. And I'm convinced that you're part of that miracle." Bill signed off, leaving Nick to reflect on that profound statement. An unborn child needed a miracle, a miracle he might contribute some small measure of expertise to ensure.

Maybe it's time you go back to the operating room, Doc. Dusty's words came back to him. Dusty, who never questioned his claim to have lost his medical memory. She hadn't shamed him for his refusal to practice medicine. In some strange way, she seemed to understand. Her only suggestion was, finally, that he should take back his life.

Did she know what that would mean? Could she possibly know the pressure, the addictive high that the power of healing gave him? It was frightening, yet the pull was powerful. Did he dare return after what had happened?

Yes. She was right. It was time. Looking back, he knew that he'd already begun. The Heimlich maneuver. Treating Dusty's wound. Examining the little boy at the Children's Center and recognizing his bruises as abuse. Reading the X rays in Bill's office. From the moment Dusty had come into his life, he'd started down a road he'd thought impassable.

Then, the night before, he'd opened himself up to a personal relationship which pushed him toward the possibility of tomorrow.

All the barriers weren't down, but he'd made a start. In loving Dusty, for the first time in a long time, he'd reached for something personal, something that had nothing to do with being a doctor.

Nick poured the rest of his coffee into the sink and rinsed his cup. There was a lot of pretty heavy stuff rolling around inside his head. It was time to take his usual Sunday morning walk around the lake. As he slipped out the back door, he stopped, inclined his head as he thought about the woman sleeping upstairs, then closed the door and locked it behind him.

He'd managed to fill his mind with ghosts and the return of his memory, avoiding any speculation over what a future with Dusty might mean. Nothing about their being together had promised a long-term relationship. Was she even interested in one?

He'd have to think about that. All he was certain of was that she was important to him. He wanted her in ways that he couldn't begin to define. The physical need was only a part of why he was drawn to Dusty. More than that, there was a connection of spirit that transcended all this ghost business.

A feeling of hope.

First he had to think about Bill and the surgery. The child didn't have much time. He and Dusty had the rest of their lives. The baby and the surgery would take his full concentration, then he and Dusty would talk about Hattie's ghosts.

Nick had come full circle, back to Hattie and her crazy suggestion she'd be back. The spiritual vortex swirling around him and Dusty was somehow connected to both Hattie and the tour. Dusty's presence and her storytelling blackouts were a part of the storm, an unsettling part.

Nick could deal with mental aberrations on his own, for he'd learned to accept that the mind could play strange tricks. But he was acutely uncomfortable with the signs he was seeing in Dusty. She seemed to become the woman in the ghost story, absorbing unseen messages of some kind as she spoke. The people on the tour thought she was very good, but Nick was convinced that once she started telling the story, she became Danielle. At the end, Dusty still insisted that her swoon was part of her presentation, but he wasn't convinced.

Then there were the dreams, the one she seemed to be having while he held her after the last rehearsal and his own imagined reincarnations of the woman in the hip bath. It was becoming far too easy to see himself in the picture with Dusty.

All his dreams were different. Before Dusty came he'd dreamed about the wreck, about Lois, and about dark caverns of pure nothingness. Everything in his dreams had been still and dead, no sound, no color, only pain. But everything had changed. Slashes of color, turmoil, waves of flame and heat and passion had changed the darkness into pleasure beyond description.

Dear God, the passion was like a raging inferno, carrying him into physical release even in his dreams. The people in the reverie weren't him and Dusty, and yet they were. It was all such a wild, uncontrolled fantasy. He might as well be fourteen instead of thirty-four.

So, he rationalized, he had the hots for Dusty. But he'd made love to her and it hadn't changed anything—except to fan the fragile ray of hope that kept nudging him forward. It was all he could do to keep himself from turning around and climbing those stairs and loving her again.

Even at the height of their passion, he knew that his need was more than just lust. He liked the woman. He liked being with her. She didn't expect anything except honesty, and she gave that same honesty in return. More, beneath all that street-smart savvy and lush beauty, she was fragile. She'd been hurt, and she'd struck out.

He'd been hurt, and he'd turned the hurt inside.

Now they'd come together, seeking solace from a kindred spirit. Would it be possible for two people so totally different to find a common ground?

He groaned. They'd already found a common ground. What they needed was a normal one. What he needed was an emotional textbook, a procedural manual, some kind of instructions that told him how to blow away the smoke and help him see the sunlight.

Nick drove to the place he normally parked his car and began to jog. He let out a bitter laugh. Even Bill would smirk at his clumsy attempt at running. Still, he was growing stronger and his legs were steadier than before. Even now as he moved down the sidewalk, beneath the crown of autumn leaves and chirping birds, he felt a curious peace settle over him.

Reaching down, he drew on an inner strength that had always seen him through times of fear and exhaustion. It was still there, feeding the needs of his soul. His steps became surer, stronger, and the sunlight warmed him.

If Bill were watching, he might not see the

smoothness of Nick's stride, but Nick felt it. He was running slowly but surely toward the lake, the sound of the carillon bells drawing him along.

Maybe, just maybe, he was coming back to life.

Tomorrow called to him, challenged him. Tomorrow would bring the first test of his medical skills in more than a year.

Dr. Nick Elliott would spend the next few days preparing, then he'd go to surgery and assist in a miracle.

Desirée stood before the mirror and studied the woman looking back at her. Gone was Officer O'Brian. Gone was Dusty, the protective street kid. Gone was the rebellious teenager who'd run away in the middle of the night and the resigned woman who'd hitched a ride from Florida to Georgia.

The person she saw was simply a woman, a woman who'd been made love to by a man. Her hair was tousled. Her nude body was flushed and aching. Under her gaze, her nipples hardened and moved up and down as her breathing came faster. She didn't recognize the woman she was seeing, and that scared her.

Always before, she'd been sure of what and who she was. She might never know where she was going, or allow herself to feel any regret about what she'd left behind, but she knew at any given moment in her life who she was at that time.

Now she was all new. The woman with the big blue-gray eyes was a stranger, a new entity reforming herself within the invisible framework of the past. For the first time in her life there was a weak but valiant light struggling to survive out there in the dark future.

All because of Hattie.

No, it went deeper than that. Because of Nick.

Dusty ran her fingertips across her swollen lips, parting them instinctively, allowing the quick hot breath she'd been holding to escape.

"Thank you, Hattie, for sending me my own wizard."

There was no answer, only a kind of waiting. She was alone. There was no one in the house but Dusty, not even an errant spirit ready to tease or to interfere.

When she'd awakened and found Nick gone, she'd felt sudden fear. Then she wondered what she would have felt if he'd still been there. It would have been awkward. What did one say to a lover who had to be a one-night stand? "It was a nice start to the rest of my life. How about one more for the road?"

She'd wanted the man's body, been intensely drawn to him from the first. It had been her decision to sleep with him and get past that attraction so that they could deal with Hattie's strange bequests.

Now she'd done it. Now reality could set in. But he'd been the one to get up and go home, back to his own room—wherever. That saved embarrassment for them both. Now, as soon as she got a shower and washed the powerful smell of him from her body, she'd formulate a way to get on with the rest of her life.

Dusty walked naked out of the bedroom and down the corridor to the bathroom. There were water marks on the shower stall. Unlike his usual neat self, Nick had flung a wet towel carelessly over the rack. He'd showered before he went wherever he'd gone.

As she stepped beneath the hot spray, she wondered if he smelled her on his skin, if he'd stood before the mirror in wonder at the change one night had made in his life? No, that was a woman thing, she decided. Soaping her body, she forced herself to replay the events of the night. Closing them off only allowed them to grow in potency. Only by examining them could she take away the mystery, the wonder.

Only this time it didn't work that way. With every swipe of the washcloth her body responded, not to her touch, but to the memory of Nick's. She wasn't removing memories; she was anticipating new ones.

"Sweet heaven, this isn't helping, Dusty.

You're not taking charge of your future, you're just turning yourself on."

Future. The one thing she'd vowed never to acknowledge. Her future had always been decimated in one way or another by those she thought cared about her, beginning with the father who left before she'd been born. If her mother knew who he was, she would never talk about him, only that he never said good-bye. Her mother had never said good-bye either. Neither had Martha.

Hattie had loved her unconditionally. Dusty had always known that, even when she'd hated her adoptive aunt for her plan to send her away to boarding school. It wasn't that Dusty didn't want to go to the school, it was that she refused to let Hattie leave her.

Dusty had decided early on that if Desirée O'Brian was going to be left alone again, she'd be the one to go first, before someone else did the leaving.

Poor Hattie. Dear Hattie who never gave up, who, in the end, found a way to force Dusty to come back and face the truth. Hattie, who'd sent Nick to make it easier for Dusty to face her past.

Now Nick had gone.

Dear Nick. Dusty would never, could never, be the kind of woman for a man like him. Sooner or later he'd get back to the life he was meant to live, she couldn't change that.

Nick hadn't said good-bye either.

She ought to get out of there. *Yes, that's the thing to do. Pack up and hit the road. Now, before he comes back. If he comes back.*

She turned off the shower, dried herself, and dressed. Throwing her few possessions into her backpack, she dashed down the stairs and out the kitchen door.

Moments later she was riding her bicycle toward the village, coming to a stop as a car pulled into the parking lot beside the ART Station.

"Dusty?"

David Thomas's voice stopped her. "Where are you heading?" he asked.

"I—I'm just out for a Sunday ride. What are you doing here? Do you work seven days a week?"

"Nope, came down to help get our art teacher's van loaded up for Monday's class at the Children's Center, since Nick can't go with her."

"Nick's not going?"

"No. He called a while ago and asked me if I'd fill in. And since there will be so many things going on tomorrow, I thought I'd better get ready this afternoon."

Dusty felt the breath rush out of her lungs. She knew that until this moment she hadn't really believed that Nick was leaving. But he was. He'd even called David to find a replacement for him.

So, he wasn't bound by Hattie's will to continue his work with the Station. He could pack up and go home, if that was what he wanted.

Damn him. He could have said good-bye. A man didn't just make love to a woman and disappear. But he hadn't implied that he'd see her through the storytelling, and she had no right to expect him to be there.

Dusty felt a wave of panic overtake her. The following night she was supposed to tell the story again. Dusty wasn't sure whether the panic came because of what had happened before or because there was a possibility that Nick wouldn't be there in the corner giving her the courage to tell Hattie's ghost story.

"Is Nick leaving—permanently?" she asked.

"I don't know. I didn't ask. Didn't he tell you?"

"No," she admitted. "But I haven't seen him since—last night. David, could I go with the artist tomorrow?"

David looked at her with an odd expression on his face. "Well, okay. We always welcome all the help we can get. Are you sure? I mean, even Hattie never went into the Children's Center classroom."

"I'm sure. There was a time when Hattie thought I had some artistic talent. I just spent years trying to ignore it."

"Well, Thelma leaves here about nine

o'clock. She'll get you back in time to rest up for the spooks."

Dusty nodded, rode her bike off down the road, and turned it back toward the house. She'd done enough leaving in her life. Maybe it wouldn't make things any different, but she thought that she might give staying a chance. Tomorrow wasn't really the future. She was morally obligated to stay a week, and she'd take it one day at a time.

If Merlin left, so be it. She'd make it on her own.

"Aunt Hattie, if you're listening, you'd better be prepared to step in and give me moral support. In fact, maybe you'd better materialize and tell the story yourself. Hell's bells, send me Mother Goose. I could use her help."

"Dusty darling," Hattie's voice spoke out as easily as if she were riding on the back of Dusty's bike. "You don't need anybody. You never did. But it is nice having someone who can share the uncertainty."

Dusty tightened her grip on the bars. "I don't know how you do this, Hattie, but I'm beginning to believe that you aren't a figment of my imagination."

"That's what Nicky said, just a few minutes ago. He's got to turn himself around and get back, but he's got a few problems to work out first. Be patient, Dusty, love is as hard to accept as it is to give."

The sound of distant bells came floating through the air. Hattie's neighbor on the other side of the street had hung a sheet from a tree, creating a ghost that fluttered in the breeze. Pumpkins garnished every porch like squatty candles on a birthday cake. Halloween was only a week away, and Dusty wasn't sure whether to believe Hattie or not.

She was having trouble deciding whether love was a trick or a treat.

ELEVEN

Hattie didn't cause any more manifestations to occur.

Nick didn't come home until after Dusty was asleep.

When Dusty arrived at the Station the next morning, Thelma was ready to go. By lunchtime Dusty had learned more about the humanitarian side of Dr. Nick Elliott than she'd ever expected.

"You mean he's been examining the children while you teach them?"

"Not in the beginning, only in the last week. I thought at first it was because he was someone who was concerned, but now I think it's because he's had some special kind of training."

"Of course he has," Dusty said, "he's a doctor."

Disbelief swept across the teacher's face. "Really? That explains why the center had him sign those forms."

It was Dusty's turn to be surprised. "You mean you didn't know he was a doctor?"

"No, he never said, and I never asked. I just knew it was unusual to find a man who related to the children so well. And then when he began to notice things about them, to help them, I was grateful. He seemed so lonely."

"Do you know where he is this morning?" Dusty asked.

"No. David didn't say."

The art classes were fun. The enthusiasm of the students was contagious, and by the time Dusty and the art teacher returned to the Station, Dusty had discovered that she had more artistic talent than she knew. That, and a certain natural empathy she'd always considered one of her strong points as a police officer, made her efforts a success.

On their return to the Station, Dusty was invited to accompany Thelma again, and she agreed, providing Nick approved. She hurried home, already formulating suggestions about how they might expand the ART Station's efforts.

"Nick?"

The house was empty. Really empty.

A note was propped against the toaster.

Dusty. I have something I have to do for the next couple of days. I'm sorry to desert you. Just pretend Hattie is there and you'll tell her story fine.

Merlin

Merlin? He signed the note Merlin. Why? Where had he gone so suddenly? What had she done to scare him away? She knew that she'd been pretty wild in bed with Nick, letting go with a freedom she had never experienced, but it never occurred to her that he'd panic and jump ship.

Obviously he took her at her word: Sleep together, take care of the urge, and get past sex and desire. Apparently it had worked for him. Why hadn't it worked for her? Here she was standing in the middle of a kitchen, the one room in the house in which she'd spent little time, and she felt a pool of heat puddling in her lower body.

A no-brainer, that's what this was, an exercise in futility. A letdown. A pain in the . . . heart. Dusty turned and climbed the stairs. Nick's shaving gear was gone from the bathroom. She didn't know how many clothes he normally kept in the closet, but there was a blank space to indicate that some were missing.

Gone. Nick was really gone. Even the suggestion of Hattie's presence was gone, and Dusty needed her. Dusty stood by the window and emptied her mind, just as Aunt Hattie had instructed her to do so long ago.

"Let the mind flow free," she'd said, "and your answer will come."

Except this time nothing happened.

This time her mind was a dark, cold place, as it had been in prison. She'd been better off to stay in Florida, rather than find Nick and lose him.

Odd, the idea of her having been in prison hadn't bothered him. He'd even suggested that she go back and try to clear her name. But when she'd left Florida, she'd sworn that she'd never set foot back there again. She had no reason to. Only pain and disappointment waited there.

"Pain is like your footprint in the sand," a voice that sounded eerily like Hattie's said, "the one you left behind. The only way to make new prints is to erase the old ones. You have to wipe the sand clear, Dusty. Walk a new path."

"I can't," Dusty whispered. "I have nowhere to go."

Dusty rode to the park early with Betty. She marveled at the beehive of activity now that all the participants had gathered for the first night of the tour.

One of the buildings by the exit gate had been turned into a gift shop, selling books, Halloween candy, and the little black Adopt-a-Ghost boxes tied up with the curly orange ribbon.

One group of guild members had set up a refreshment stand where they would serve hot cider, brownies, and popcorn.

The bevy of tour guides joined the storytellers in the costume house and dressed in their period costumes. The lanterns were lit and everyone took their proper place; the guides to the gate, and the storytellers to their assigned spots. There would be several tours. Dusty hadn't realized that she'd have to tell the story over and over.

More nervous than she'd ever been in her life, she stood beneath the mantle and studied the woman in the portrait.

"I don't know whether you have anything to do with my story or not," she whispered to the woman, "but if you do, forgive me if I mess it up. I don't know what in hell I'm doing here anyway."

For a moment she stared at the woman, then realized that the corners of her mouth seemed to be drawn narrower than usual. Following the path of her gaze, Dusty got the distinct impression that she was focused on the broach.

"This? Is this bothering you?"

Dusty unpinned the piece of jewelry and studied it, comparing it to the piece in the painting. It was the same. If the picture hadn't verified it, the heat that emanated from the broach would have.

Then she understood. She'd pinned it to the

wrong shoulder. As she transferred it to the other side, she heard the approach of the first group of visitors.

Quickly taking her proper place, she glanced anxiously at the empty spot in the corner where Nick had stood, the spot now vacant. She cringed. Without Nick, she wasn't going to be able to do it.

"Yes you are, Dusty. Empty your mind. You know how it's done."

"Hattie?"

But it wasn't Hattie's voice that answered. The first guide had arrived and was instructing the group to divide and stand in the two roped-off doorways.

Murmurings and muted conversation came to a stop as Dusty stepped forward, eyes closed, waiting. When she finally began to speak, the words came, not inspired as before, but from memory of her past rehearsals. When she collapsed as she'd done the other times, it was dramatic, but it wasn't involuntary. Tonight she wasn't Danielle, she was Dusty, telling the story.

Still, the end result was the same. The group moved away quietly, uneasily down the stairs to the front, where they listened to the final tale of the circuit rider whose body wouldn't stay put.

Three more tours were presented before the long evening ended and Dusty was allowed to remove her costume. She was left shaken and disappointed. There was no reason for her to have expected Nick to come, but she had. All the way back to the house she held on to a faint hope that he'd be there waiting for her.

He wasn't.

Dusty couldn't sleep. She couldn't eat. Nothing felt right. Since Nick had left, every sound seemed magnified in the silent, empty house. Poor Hattie. Dusty knew that Hattie must have felt the same when she'd run away.

Each evening Dusty added a bit of longing to her story. Danielle was becoming more and more distraught and the tour more and more mesmerized by the tale. Dusty might have gotten through the tempestuous events had it not been for the growing identification she felt with the woman who was waiting for her lover to come home to her.

She was dressed and standing in her usual spot, saying a silent prayer of thanks that this was the last night. Nick still hadn't returned, and she had no inkling why he'd left or if he was coming back. She had, she admitted, accomplished her goal: to sleep with the man in the hope of getting past the attraction.

Except it hadn't worked. She wanted him. She wanted him back in her arms, in her bed, in her future. And that was what she'd been wrestling with—the possiblity of a future. Nick had suggested that she go back and clear her name.

Maybe her past was too much for him to deal with.

No, she reasoned. If she went back, it had to be for her. It was time she stopped pretending she was tough. She wasn't. Every time something bad happened, she ran away.

Until now. Telling a ghost story over and over every night was enough to make her run away. But she hadn't. She'd stuck it out. Danielle deserved to have her story told, and Dusty was determined to do it.

"They're running a little late tonight," David's voice said from the corridor. "It's begun to rain and that means we have to wait for them to run to the car for umbrellas."

"David, tell me what's upstairs?"

"Just two bedrooms, nothing more."

"Does one of the bedrooms have a fireplace and a window overlooking the river?" she asked.

"There is no river," David answered, giving her an odd look. "Of course, the house was moved to the park from its original site."

"There was a river—once." Dusty heard her own words and had no idea where they'd originated. "I mean there probably was, wherever the house was standing before."

"Well, there could have been. But I don't know about the fireplace. The room has been padlocked ever since I've been coming here. The lock's so rusty it would have to be cut off to get in."

"That's what Nick said. Why haven't those rooms been restored."

"I don't know. The stairs are pretty narrow, and it's my guess that they used those rooms for storage and for the servants."

"No. That was my private room. The room where I waited. The room where Nick will come."

The voice spoke inside Dusty's mind as clearly as if the speaker was standing beside her. It was Danielle's voice. But why would she call her husband Nick? His name was Clay.

The answer didn't come, only a cold chill that wasn't caused by the rain or by the gloom. Moments later the first group arrived, and Dusty began her tale.

By nine o'clock Dusty was exhausted. She felt tense, keyed up as never before, as if she were the one waiting for her husband. She took a moment before the last group arrived to walk to the window and lean against it. The weight of her gown seemed to pull at her shoulders. She felt a tightness in her chest and tears threatening to spill over from her eyes.

Where was Nick? She wanted him to come back, to hold her close, to make her feel safe again. She wanted his arms around her and his lips against hers.

There was a sound, and she turned just as the

artificial flame in the large candle went out, throwing the corner where Nick usually stood into total darkness.

She glanced around the room, but there was no one there.

Then the last group entered the corridor and arranged themselves in the two doorways.

"Clear your minds," she began as always. "And let the past become the present.

"My name is Danielle. I live here, at Blessing House, the house my husband built for us before the war. My husband, Nick, was so proud when he rode away to fight for our way of life. But now he's missing. 'Wait for me,' he said."

Dusty turned toward her audience as if she were letting them in on the secret.

"They tell me he's dead, but I won't believe that. No, he would never leave me. I feel him here, in my heart." Dusty tilted her head. "He will be here. Listen. There, do you hear them? Hoofbeats? I hear them every night, but Nick never comes. Nick? Nick?"

Tonight Dusty's words were different. But the pain and the anguish were the same. She again raised her eyes to the window, then dropped her head as before, tears rolling unbidden down her cheeks.

"I'm here," a male voice said from the shadows.

There was not a sound, not a movement from the crowd. They hadn't heard the voice.

"Where are you, Nick? I can't see you. Speak to me. Tell me what to do."

As she beseeched him with her eyes, she felt a veil of shadows fall between them. Nick or Clay? She knew he was there. Was it Danielle who felt the presence or Dusty? The room fell away. She tilted her head, as though she were still listening. A new room began to take shape and form.

Once more the walls turned to windows. On one side there was a bed with a red satin spread. The smell of honeysuckle seemed caught in the air currents swirling about the room. The sound of drums, of cannon fire, and of shots faded away, and then she saw him standing there, her beloved.

"Nick."

"It's me, Danielle. I've come back at last."

As he reached out for her, the grief-stricken woman took a step toward the man she loved, felt her arms touch the firm flesh of a man, of the soldier she'd waited for so long, and collapsed in a swoon.

There was a woman's cry.

This time the woman was Danielle.

"Where'd the man come from?" one visitor asked as they followed their guide out of the house.

"There was nobody there," another argued. "It was just the lightning."

"Yeah," a third one agreed. "A shadow. You could see the wall right through him."

"Naw! It was a hologram, like in *Star Trek*."

"I saw it." The voices continued to argue in hushed tones.

"Maybe," a little girl said softly as she glanced back at the man lifting the lady from where she'd fallen, "it really was a ghost. Maybe Nick finally came home."

"It it really you, Nick?" Dusty asked.

"It's me."

"Where have you been? I thought you'd left me."

"I'll never leave you, Dusty. I had something I had to do, something you told me to do. Are you all right?"

"I am now," she said with a sigh of contentment.

"Let's get out of here." He unhooked the rope and moved into the corridor.

"Not yet, Nick. There is something I have to do first."

"What?"

"Please, I want to go upstairs."

"Why? It's dark up there."

"I have to go. We have to go." Dusty's voice became frantic, almost shrill. "I don't know why or how, I just know."

Nick hesitated. Telling these stories had been

too much for Dusty. She was bordering on hysteria. "I told you there is nothing there. The rooms are padlocked."

"Put me down and I'll go alone. I won't leave without knowing."

"No, I'll take you." He turned her in his arms so that her skirt could clear the bannister and, bad leg suddenly strong, he started to climb. At the landing midway, the stairs turned back over the hallway. As they climbed, Dusty's breathing grew slower. There was a dim light at the top of the steps. It seemed to come from inside one of the rooms.

The door was open, the padlock gone. A fire crackled merrily in the fireplace. Dusty squirmed from his grasp, stepped into the room, and walked toward the window. There was a shadow, a silhouette of a woman.

Dusty felt an odd sensation steal over her, as if she had been there before, as if she'd glanced out the same window night after night, waiting for him to come.

When she reached the shadow, she recognized the woman, Danielle. Only half real, she cast a beseeching look at Dusty, then almost in a whisper said, "Please. Once more."

Suddenly Dusty felt the woman's touch, felt her shadow presence flow over her own body, the merging of the spirit and flesh, and suddenly Danielle was gone. Yet she wasn't. For as Dusty turned, she felt the sudden acceleration of her own heartbeat.

Another voice spoke through Dusty's lips. "I knew you'd come back, Nick. I've waited for so long, my darling. Please kiss me."

Nick looked around, confused. He couldn't explain the fire, or the bed, or the strange manifestation he'd witnessed. The woman he was seeing was Dusty and yet she wasn't.

"Dusty, what's wrong? What's happening?" Nick crossed the wood floor, stumbling on his injured leg, the hollow sound of his footsteps vanishing as he reached her side.

Dusty looked up at the dark, serious face she'd yearned to see, the real flesh-and-blood man she wanted. For a moment the scar on his face seemed fresh, red, puckered. She was seeing him the way he was when he'd been badly injured. "You came back. I've been so lonely, Nick. Why didn't you come back?"

"I did, Dusty. Everything is all right, finally. Because of you."

The fire blazed up and the door slowly closed.

Dusty's beautiful face turned soft with yearning. Her lips parted and her head tilted back, inviting him to reach them. Nick felt as if they were caught up in some kind of dreamlike spell. None of it made any sense. But from the moment this woman had come into his life, she'd touched it with magic.

She'd called him Merlin. Merlin the magician, who cast spells and created illusions.

Ilusions of love. Nick finally knew what it meant to love, to want to give, to need someone, to believe in tomorrow. What happened next was beyond his control. He'd opened the door and stepped through. Now it was time he stopped questioning his miracle. He lowered his head to touch the lips he'd hungered for.

He swept her into his arms and walked toward the bed, collapsing across it with such need that where and who they were fell away. His clothes were gone, as was her costume. He ripped the net from her hair and let the silver strands fall free across the scarlet spread.

"I love you," he said as he planted kisses on her face and neck. "I didn't know what love was until I met you. I didn't know it could be so powerful, so strong, so safe."

"I know," she whispered, pressing herself eagerly against him. "I've waited for you and this. I came here to love you, only you, for always."

And then he was inside her, feeling the velvet heat of her tighten around him, caressing with spasms of fire. She was moaning, whispering little words of love, of promise. He could only hold on and let the heat build until they shattered into a thousand pieces of stardust.

"Is this real?" he asked.

"It's as real as we want it to be," she said, and

pulled him closer. "We'll never let go now that we've found each other again."

"Never," he said, and felt a smoky swirl of images begin around him, of Dusty's face, of the plantation. An eerie sound of sweet music began to emanate from the veil of smoke. And the room disappeared as they moved together once more.

"Ah, Merlin, you create such beautiful magic."

TWELVE

The morning sun threw spears of gold through the window and across Nick's bed, brushing his face with harsh stripes of light and dark.

Dusty raised herself up and studied the dangerous beauty of the man who'd turned her world bright and new. She couldn't keep herself from touching him, from placing her lips against his and claiming a first kiss of a new morning, of their future.

When his arms slipped around her, she moved willingly over him, marveling once more in the feel of their bodies touching.

"Hello, magic man," she said, giving in to the strong urge to kiss him. "Why did you leave me without saying anything?"

"I knew that if I didn't go right then, without ever coming back to the house, I might not have gone through with it."

"With what? Where have you been?"

"My memory returned. I'm a doctor again."

"Oh, Nick, I'm so proud. But I don't understand why you couldn't share your hapiness with me."

"It wasn't that," he said. "Bill, my associate at the hospital, had asked me to assist in a very delicate piece of surgery. I couldn't trust myself. I was afraid I'd fail, and it was too important—to us. I needed to study, to review the procedure, to prepare."

"I understand that. Like an undercover operation. You have to concentrate all your energies on your plan, without outside interference. How did it go?"

"We did it, Dusty. We removed a tumor from a fetus without ever separating it from the mother's womb. And the baby lived. I didn't save my child, but I helped save the life of another unborn child. It was a miracle."

"Of course you did," she said softly, and kissed him again. "I told you that a wizard always makes miracles. You made one last night."

"Last night?" He opened his eyes and took a quick look around the room in which he'd spent the last months. It was exactly as it ought to be.

"What are you looking for?"

"I wanted to be sure where we are. After the dream I had last night, I'm not sure I can even trust my eyes."

"The dream? But last night we . . . we were . . ."

Then she didn't know. The last thing she remembered was the stairs. "You were there, weren't you, in the darkness while I was telling the story?"

"Yes, I slipped in when the lights went out."

"And afterward, we went up the stairs, to the room with the scarlet spread. Don't you remember?"

Nick frowned. "I'm not sure I understand what I'm remembering. What was real and what was in the dream? You've bewitched me, wildcat."

Dusty laid her head against his chest, listening for the rapid beat of his heart. "Now I'm not sure. Was it a dream, Nick? I don't think so."

"You really don't believe that we made love up there in that locked room, do you?"

"I don't know," she answered, "but something happened. Danielle was there. I'm sure. She was waiting for her husband, as she had been for over a hundred years. She was waiting for you, Nicholas."

"Me?"

"She thought so. And you came back to her. Don't you see? The waiting for her is over. She —they can be together forever, just like us."

"I like the sound of that *us* part," he said, nuzzling her throat and moving his fingertips across her back.

"Together. We'll stay right here, in Hattie's house—unless you'd rather move back to your house?" She lifted her head and looked at him, waiting for a reply.

"That was never my house. I'll sell it and donate the money to—"

"The ART Station, for their school program. Nick, I went with the teacher, and I learned what she does. It's a remarkable thing, watching those children learn about beauty and how to create it."

"Yes," Nick agreed, "I think Hattie would have liked your taking part in the program."

"And you'll go back to practicing medicine?" Dusty asked.

"I've already told Bill that I was coming back. Except this time we're going to work on perfecting laser surgery on infants. I won't make as much money as I did in private practice, but if we can make it work, the rewards will be enormous."

The door suddenly slammed. Dusty looked around. "What was that?"

"I think Siggy was announcing his departure."

"My ghost?"

Nick didn't elaborate. Someday he'd explain to Dusty about the odd man in the out-of-date black coat, but not now. For now, he just wanted to be with Dusty, touch her, feel the fire surge to life within.

He could tell from the heavy look in Dusty's eyes that she was having a hard time keeping her mind on the conversation. Nick wasn't doing any better. The forward-moving part of his body was keeping pace with his plans for the future on an accelerated level.

"Your ghost, or at least one of them," Nick replied, and gave himself over to an example of total involvement. He didn't want to think that Sigmund Freud and Hattie had been watching. Then he decided that he didn't care. Besides, knowing Hattie, she probalby brought Dr. Freud back for very personal reasons.

Later as they ate strawberries and Critter cereal, Nick voiced the thought that had been nudging at his mind since he'd waked.

"Dusty, I have to run over to the plantation this morning. I won't be long. Would you mind?"

"I would. I just got you back and I'm not letting you out of my sight. I'll go with you. What are we going to do?"

"Just walk the tour route and make sure that nothing is left out of order. The caretaker will get his nose out of joint if he has to make any repairs after us."

"Well, let's get to it. I have a couple of things I have to take care of myself."

Nick stood, planted a kiss behind Dusty's ear

that threatened their immediate departure, then gave a sigh of regret and placed their cereal bowls in the sink.

A short time later they arrived at the park, parked the car at the gate, and entered the plantation acreage.

Dusty was content to meander along, holding Nick's hand, enjoying the clear blue sky and the warm autumn morning. He stopped here and there, examining a fence post or a barn door. They finally reached the house, entering from the lower level on the side.

As they climbed the steps to the first floor, Dusty took Nick's hand, holding it tightly. "The house feels different," she said. "Can you tell?"

"I'm not sure. It's quiet and it's cool."

They walked past the stairs leading up and stopped at the entrance to the drawing room.

"It's at peace. Look at the portrait, Nick. It's changed."

Nick unhooked the rope and walked into the room, studying the painting.

"You're right. Her hair seems darker and her eyes—"

"They don't follow you anymore. Oh, Nick. It's true. She's gone. Danielle isn't here anymore."

Nick nodded. He understood that feeling of peace. Once they'd finished the baby's surgery and its heart had remained strong, he'd felt that quiet serenity. He was willing to concede that miracles could happen. Later, when the mother had opened her eyes and whispered, "Thank you," he'd been certain.

"I don't begin to understand any of this," he said, "but I believe something good happened here."

As they turned away from the room, they were facing the stairs leading up. Dusty didn't hesitate. She started to climb them.

"Are you sure you want to go up there?" he asked. "Sometimes it's better not to know."

At the top of the stairs she stopped, leaned down, and picked up something from the floor. "You're right," she said softly. "Some things are best left untouched."

She tucked the object she'd found in her pocket and turned back to the man who had brought sunlight and stardust back into her life.

"Let's go, Merlin, and make some more magic of our own."

It was the next week when Dusty and Nick lay in bed looking out at the night sky that the ghost box fell off the dressing table where it had been for several days.

Dusty rose and picked it up again. The box wouldn't stay in one place. She finally decided that, as the instructions had warned, Siggy was unhappy, and he was making his feelings known.

Siggy, Hattie, and Dusty. They all had something to do, and Dusty was just putting her chore off. Nick was back at the hospital. Dusty had begun accompanying the art teacher every day. But that wasn't enough. The time had come to make her own commitment to their future.

"What's wrong?" Nick asked, pulling himself up to the head of the bed and watching her. "I know you, wildcat, and something's bothering you."

"Yes. I have to go back to Florida, Nick, to clear my name."

He'd been expecting something, but now that it had come he wasn't prepared for her leaving.

"Nick, you've conquered your demons. You've filled the black places in your mind with stardust, but I'm still carrying around my past."

"You know you weren't guilty of any crime and, trust me, darling, nobody else cares. If you don't want to go back, don't."

She didn't know how to tell him, for she hadn't quite worked it out herself. But her life was still messed up. By letting things stand, she would always feel that she didn't deserve Nick. But she couldn't put it into words, resorting instead to the kind of smart remark he might expect.

"You know me," she quipped, "I'm good at leaving."

That he hadn't expected. Neither had their resident ghosts. This time the box sailed off the bureau, barely missing Dusty's head.

"Fine. I'll give you three months," Hattie's voice cut through the silence. "I'll even go with you."

Dusty turned toward Nick. "Did you hear that?"

"I heard. I saw. If that box had been a couple of inches to the left, I would have felt it. And you're not good at leaving, not anymore. Look at you, standing there in the buff like some siren tempting me into becoming a love slave. Your feet are glued to the floor."

He knew he was grinning. He wondered what Bill would say if Nick told him that he lived with a spirit in a haunted house, then decided that Bill would probably believe it.

"Oh, Nick," she said, moving back into his arms. "Staying would be easy. I don't want to go. I want to be here with you and be loved forever, but I can't, not yet."

"Then I'll go with you," Nick said. "After all, you can use the help of a wizard."

"No, I have to do this on my own. Besides, Hattie will come along."

Nick groaned. "I always thought ghosts had to stay in one place, that they were tied to their past. How come our resident spook is mobile?"

"I think she's tied to us. Wherever we go, she goes. Besides, I'll make it easy. I'll take the box." She grinned. "I figure I have at least a four-month supply of ghost food left."

"I thought your tag said a year."

"That was for one. My box seems to be home for two."

Nick laughed. "Hattie Lanier and Dr. Freud, do you suppose . . . ?"

As it turned out, Dusty didn't have to stay in Florida long. The men who'd framed her had since decided that it had been so easy, they'd expand their acitvities to accepting bribes for turning a blind eye to drug dealers.

They might have gone on forever, except they stole evidence from the crime storage room and covered their latest act by framing a federal agent who was working undercover in the police department. One of the guilty officers agreed to turn state's evidence against the others, and the ring of crooked cops came crashing down.

Officials were skeptical about their informant's strange story that he was visited by the Ghost of Crimes Past—an odd-looking man in a black suit—and the Ghost of Crimes Present—a woman in a red dress. After the informant explained that the ghosts urged him to clear Dusty O'Brian, the Chief of Police advised him to forget the ghosts and simply tell what happened.

The truth was readily accepted by those officers who never believed that Dusty was guilty.

The prosecutor quickly asked the judge to clear Dusty's record of any wrongdoing and reinstate her to the force with full pay for the time she'd spent in jail.

Dusty turned down the chance to return to her job and donated her salary to the benevolent organization whose funds she'd been accused of embezzling.

For the first time in more than two years, Dusty O'Brain was a free woman, free to follow her heart. She took the next flight back to Nick.

Inside her carry-on, Dusty had carefully cushioned the shiny black ghost box, securing it with underwear and cosmetics so that it wouldn't bounce around. Away from the sensual overtones that constantly jammed her normal thinking processes, she'd made up her mind what she and Nick had to do.

Hattie had said it best long ago. The best way to get rid of the dark spaces is to fill them with stardust.

Dusty was nervous. Although Nick had told her that he loved her, returning to their little house was a risk. Suppose he'd changed his mind? Suppose he'd decided that they weren't really suited? Suppose he . . . ?

"Suppose you get us home and find out before you go asking for trouble. Watch it Siggy, get your elbow out of my back."

Dusty looked quickly at the other travelers, wondering if they'd heard Hattie's voice. The man on the left was dozing, and the one on the right was reading a magazine. Apparently she was the only one who'd heard the voice.

Silently she admonished her secret companions, and they remained silent the rest of the way. From the airport she caught the transit system train to the closest stop to the Station, then took a taxi to the house.

The empty house.

There was no way Nick could have known when she'd arrive, since she hadn't told him that she was coming home. After arranging the ghost box on the table in the parlor, she went upstairs, her heart in her throat until she comfirmed that his clothing ws still in his closet.

Once she knew he hadn't gone, she hurried to unpack and plan how she would greet him with her news. Nothing in her closet was right. Nothing was romantic enough. Nothing said, "I'm yours, take me."

It was back to Hattie's costume room. She found a rack of satin caftans with flowing sleeves and mandarin collars. A black one was large enough to fit Nick. Perfect, she thought, and laid it out, then chose a deep purple robe cut low across the shoulders for herself.

At some point in her career, Hattie had either acted in *Camelot*, or she'd played out her fantasy of having her own personal wizard. All Dusty needed now was something for her hair, something glittery.

She began rummaging through a trunk that she hadn't opened before. Inside she found a jewelry box filled with combs, pins, and necklaces. A spray of gems interspersed with glitter was perfect. Long dangling gold-and-amethyst earrings completed the look. As she replaced the top tray she caught sight of a familiar piece of jewelry, a delicate broach made of gold and pearls.

Holding it in her hand, Dusty felt a sense of contentment steal over her. She'd seen the broach before. She'd worn it on her ballgown on the tour. It was the same as the one in the painting, the one she'd found dropped on the stairs. Now it was back in the case and she hadn't put it there.

Dusty frowned. She didn't understand. But much of what had happened defied explanation. How could Danielle, the widow who'd waited for her lover, have been wearing the broach? Danielle, the woman in Hattie's tale. Who had written the tale and passed it on to Hattie?

"Thank you, my dear," Hattie's voice said softly. "The ghost story was real. It came from my great-great-grandmother's diary, my ancestor, Danielle. Telling the story was all part of the plan to bring the lovers together at last, to close the circle, to make the past and the present complete. And you did it—for me. I always knew you would, from the first time I saw you."

Dusty understood finally why Hattie had never found her ending for the tale. She didn't, couldn't have been certain. She could only set the events into motion and wait for them to be resolved.

Wait for Danielle and Clay to find each other through Dusty and Nick. Wait for the past, the present, and the future to be made right.

"But what about you, Hattie?" Dusty said, clasping the broach in her hand. "What do you want?"

"You'll figure it out, child. You know what to do."

And Dusty did.

She placed the caftan on Nick's bed. After a quick shower she dressed, made up her face, and arranged the final portion of her plan.

By the time she heard a car pulling into the drive, she was dressed and ready. Dinner was in the oven and the table was covered with a white lace cloth, crystal wineglasses, and china plates rimmed with black and gold. And in the center of the table was the black ghost box, tied to a bunch of silver balloons with orange and black ribbon.

The sound of footsteps on the back porch announced Nick's arrival. She knew it was Nick, for the two of them were the only ones who came and went from the back of the house.

Dusty took a deep breath and switched off the overhead lights, leaving only the candles flickering in the shadows. She hoped that she hadn't made a mistake.

The door opened and Nick came to a stop, sniffing the aroma of food and—honeysuckle? He turned his head until his eyes found the silhouette of the woman standing by the table.

Dusty had come home. He hadn't been certain that she would. His heart began to thud as he walked toward her. "Hello, wildcat. I'm glad you're back. I've missed you."

Nick gathered Dusty in his arms and held her, content to feel her against him. He tangled his hands in her hair, rubbing his chin against her cheek, breathing in the lush sweet scent of the woman with whom he intended to spend the rest of his life.

"I like your outfit. It's very unusual."

"We're dressing up tonight, Merlin. You'll find something special on your bed. After we eat, will you put it on?"

"I'm more into taking off than putting on, Dusty. Could we delay dinner for just a while?"

He stole her breath with his kiss and her mind with his touch. Dinner waited. Time stopped, and a fat harvest moon rose over the treetops as Nick and Dusty made hungry love.

Later, when they'd circled the stars and returned to earth, Dusty told him what had happened.

"I'm free now, Nick. I can be with you without bringing you shame." Dusty reached up and touched the scar on his face. It had faded so that it was almost nonexistent.

Nick glared down at her, his dark eyes snapping dangerously. "I could never be ashamed of you, Desirée O'Brian. You're the most beautiful woman I've ever known, inside and out. If you were a criminal on the lam, I'd still want you."

"You would?"

"I would. I want you again, now. Do I have to tell you?"

"No," she said in a low voice, thick with passion, "just show me. I'm a sucker for a magic man."

It was very late when they donned their satin robes and ate dinner.

"Actually," Nick said, as he drained his glass and looked across the table at the woman whose eyes were filled with love, "actually, I rather like the feel of this satin against my skin. Are you sure this is what Merlin wore?"

"Well, he probably had something underneath his, but otherwise you're pretty authentic."

"And you are my helper?"

"We're a team, Merlin, from now on. Though to be a wizard's helper, I would probably have been a man."

"I'm glad you're not. When do I find out why I'm dressed like this?"

"Now. The time has come for us to send Hattie and Siggy away."

Dusty removed the broach she was wearing and held it out so that Nick could see it.

"Say, isn't that the broach in the picture, the one you wore on the tour?"

"It is."

"How—"

"Hattie arranged it. I don't know how, but it belonged to her great-great-grandmother Danielle."

Nick watched as Dusty placed the broach inside the ghost box and retied the ribbon holding the balloons.

"I don't understand," he said.

"Come with me." Dusty took Nick's hand, and they walked out the back door into the yard. "We're going to send Hattie's spirit into the heavens."

"But the top to the box, you left it inside."

"Of course. That's so the empty space inside the box can be filled with stardust. Take hold of my hand, Nick. I'd like to release it together."

Nick placed his hand over hers and together they let go, watching as the balloons sailed up into the night sky, over the treetops, toward the stars. A quick little breeze caught the ribbons, swaying the magic conveyance for a moment, then whisking it across the face of the moon.

Nick's arm went around Dusty, and she laid her head back against his shoulder.

After a long peaceful silence the speck of black disappeared into the night sky.

"Let's go inside, Nick," Dusty said. "We have to talk about what I'm going to now."

"You're going to become a police officer again," he said, "and you're going to spend the rest of your life loving me."

"I think what I want to do is work with children," she said. "Sick children, abandoned children, children in pain who need someone like Hattie in their lives."

"Do you have something in mind?"

"Maybe we could use Hattie's house for a safe haven. Those babies you operate on, their families, those who don't have anyone to care. We could take them in until they're well. Would you mind terribly, sharing Hattie's house?"

"Not with you. The solution is perfect," he said, and started toward the back door.

"No," she said, "not the back door, not anymore, Merlin. From now on, we're going in the front. Both of us. What do you say?"

Standing there, holding hands, in the shadow of the big magnolia tree that towered over the house and filled half the postage-stamp front yard, Nick knew that what Dusty was proclaiming was a lot more than just a way into the house. They were announcing to the world that they'd found their place together.

After a long moment he nodded, opened the front door, and they stepped inside. Nick switched off the porch light behind them. Only the waning glow of the candles illuminated the room.

"The smell of honeysuckle is gone," he said. "Does that mean that we'll never hear from Hattie again?"

"I don't know," Dusty replied, staring at an object in the center of the foyer. "But I think she's left us a present. Look."

It was a very old cradle made of oak, its headboard tied with orange and black ribbons. As they watched, there in the candlelight, it began to rock.

Across the trees, the plantation caretaker glanced up at the moon and caught sight of the balloons sailing past. "Who'd believe it?" he whispered as he felt a shiver ripple down his spine. "It's some kind of ghost ship, and it's headed toward the stars."

THE EDITOR'S CORNER

At this time of year there is always much to be thankful for, not the least of which are the four terrific romances coming your way next month. These stories are full of warmth, passion, and love—just the thing for those cold winter nights. So make a date to snuggle up under a comforter and read the LOVE-SWEPTs we have in store for you. They're sure to heat up your reading hours with their witty and sensuous tales.

The wonderfully talented Terry Lawrence starts things off with a hero who's **A MAN'S MAN**, LOVESWEPT #718. From the moment Reilly helps Melissa Drummond into the helicopter, she is enthralled—mesmerized by this man of mystery who makes her feel safe and threatened all at once! Sensing the needs she's long denied, he tempts her to taste desire, to risk believing in a love that will last. Once he's warned her that he'll woo her until he's won, she must trust his promises enough to vow her own. This tale of irresistible courtship is another Terry Lawrence treasure.

THE COP AND THE MOTHER-TO-BE, LOVESWEPT #719, is the newest heartwarming romance from Charlotte Hughes. Jake Flannery had shared Sammie Webster's grief at losing her husband, cared for her as her child grew inside her, and flirted with her when she knew no one could find a puffy pregnant lady sexy—but she doesn't dare wonder why this tough cop's touch thrills her. And Jake tries not to imagine making love to the feisty mom or playing daddy to her daughter. But somehow their cherished friendship has turned to dangerous desire, and Jake must pull out all the stops to get Sammie to confess she'll adore him forever. The ever popular Charlotte Hughes offers a chance to laugh and cry and fall in love all over again.

Get ready for Lynne Bryant's **DAREDEVIL,** LOVESWEPT #720. Casey Boone is Dare King's buddy, his best friend, the only girl he's ever loved—but now that he might never walk again, Dare King struggles not to let her see his panic . . . or the pain he still feels three years after she left him at the altar! Casey has never stopped loving her proud warrior but fears losing him as she'd lost her dad. Now she must find the courage to heal Dare—body and soul—at last. In this touching and sizzling novel, Lynne Bryant explores the power of love, tested but enduring.

Linda Cajio wants you to meet an **IRRESISTIBLE STRANGER,** LOVESWEPT #721. Leslie Kloslosky doesn't believe her friend's premonition that she'll meet the perfect man on her vacation in

England—right up to the instant a tall, dark stranger enters the cramped elevator and lights a fire in her blood! Fascinated by the willowy brunette whose eyes turn dark sapphire when he kisses her, Mike Smith isn't about to let her go . . . but will he be clever enough to elude a pair of thieves hot on their trail? Linda Cajio weaves a treasured romantic fantasy you won't forget.

Happy reading!

With warmest wishes,

Beth de Guzman

Senior Editor

P.S. Don't miss the women's novels coming your way in December: **ADAM'S FALL,** from blockbuster author Sandra Brown, is a deliciously sensual story of a woman torn between her duty and her heart; **PURE SIN,** from nationally bestselling author Susan Johnson, is a sensuous tale of thrilling seduction set in nineteenth-century Montana; **ON WINGS OF MAGIC,** by the award-winning Kay Hooper, is a classic contemporary romance of a woman who must make a choice between protecting her heart and surrendering to love once more. We'll be giving you a sneak peek at these wonderful books in next month's LOVESWEPTs. And immediately following this page look for a preview of the terrific romances from Bantam that are *available now!*

Don't miss these incomparable books
by your favorite Bantam authors

On sale in October

WANTED

by Patricia Potter

SCANDAL IN

SILVER

by Sandra Chastain

THE WINDFLOWER

by Sharon and Tom Curtis

Winner of the *Romantic Times* 1992
Storyteller of the Year Award

PATRICIA POTTER

NATIONALLY BESTSELLING AUTHOR OF *RELENTLESS* AND *NOTORIOUS*

WANTED

*Texas Ranger Morgan Davis hadn't grown up with much
love, but he had been raised with respect for duty and the
law. To him, Lorilee Braden was nothing but a con artist,
yet her fire and beauty drew him despite his better judgment. Still, her brother was wanted for murder—and the
face on the wanted poster looked far too much like Morgan's for comfort. The only way he could clear his own
name was to bring Nicholas Braden to justice . . . before
the spark Lori had lit became a raging blaze that consumed
everything Morgan believed in . . .*

Braden balked at moving again. "Where's my sister?"

"In back," Morgan said. He led his prisoner to the
tree several yards behind the cabin. The woman immediately saw Nicholas Braden, her eyes resting on
the handcuffs for a moment, then she glared at Morgan.

Braden stepped over to his sister, stooped down,

and awkwardly pulled the gag from her mouth. "Are you all right?"

Morgan leaned back lazily against a tree and watched every movement, every exchange of silent message between the sister and brother. He felt a stab of longing, a regret that he'd never shared that kind of caring or communication with another human being.

Braden tried to untie his sister, but the handcuffs hindered him. Morgan heard a muffled curse and saw the woman's face tense with pain.

"Move away," Morgan said to Braden. Braden hesitated.

"Dammit, I'm not going to keep repeating myself." Irritation and impatience laced Morgan's words.

Braden stood, took a few steps away.

"Farther," Morgan ordered. "Unless you want her to stay there all night."

Braden backed up several feet, and Morgan knelt beside Lorilee Braden. With the knife from his belt, he quickly cut the strips of cloth binding her. Unfamiliar guilt rushed through him as he saw blood on her wrists. He hadn't tied her that tightly, but apparently the cloth had cut into her skin when she'd struggled to free herself.

His gaze met hers, and he was chilled by the contempt there. He put out his hand to help her up, but she refused it, trying to gain footing by herself. Her muscles must have stiffened because she started to fall.

Instinctively reaching out to help her, Morgan dropped the knife, and he saw her go for it. His foot slammed down on it. Then her hand went for the gun in Braden's gunbelt, which Morgan had slung over his shoulder.

Morgan swore as he spun her around, his hand going around her neck to subdue her. Out of the corner of his eye, he saw Nicholas Braden move toward him. "Don't," Morgan said. "I might just make a mistake and hurt her."

All rage and determination, she was quivering against him, defying him with every ounce of her being.

"You do real well against women, don't you?" Braden taunted.

Morgan had always had a temper—he felt ready to explode now—but his voice was even and cold when he spoke. "You'd better tell your sister to behave herself if she wants you to live beyond this day." His arms tightened around her. She wriggled to escape his hold, and he felt his body's reaction to it. It puzzled him. It infuriated him. He didn't like what he didn't understand, and he couldn't understand his reaction to this she-cat. She was trouble, pure trouble, but a part of him admired her, and he despised that admiration as a weakness in himself. "Tell her!"

"Lori."

Braden's voice was low but authoritative, and Morgan felt the girl relax slightly, then jerk away from him and run to her brother. Braden's hand-cuffed hands went over her head and around her, and he held her as she leaned trustingly against him. A criminal. A killer. A rare wave of loneliness swept over Morgan, flooding him with intense jealousy, nearly turning him inside out.

"Touching scene," he observed sarcastically, his voice rough as he tried to reestablish control—over his prisoner and the woman and over himself.

He tried to discipline his own body, to dismiss the

lingering flowery scent of Lorilee Braden, the re-membered softness of her body against his. She was a hellion, he warned himself, not soft at all, except in body. He'd already underestimated her twice. He wouldn't do it again.

SCANDAL IN SILVER

BY

SANDRA CHASTAIN

"This delightful author has a tremendous talent that places her on a pinnacle reserved for special romance writers."—*Affaire de Coeur*

Sandra Chastain is a true reader favorite, and with SCANDAL IN SILVER, her new "Once Upon a Time Romance," she borrows from Seven Brides for Seven Brothers *for a wonderfully funny and sensual historical romance about five sisters stranded in the Colorado wilderness with a silver mine.*

"What was that?" he said, and came to a full stop.

To her credit she didn't jump up or cry out. Instead she looked around slowly, tilting her head to listen to the sounds of the night.

"I don't hear anything, Colter."

"We're being watched. Stand up slowly. Hold out your hand and smile."

She followed his directions, but the smiling was hard. She was certain there was nothing out there and that he knew it. This was a ruse. She'd known not to trust him; this proved it. "Now what?"

He returned her smile, dropped his wood and started toward her, speaking under his breath. "When I take your hand I'm going to put my arms around you and we'll walk deeper into the trees."

"Why?"

"I don't know what's going to happen, and I don't want to be out in the open." He hoped she didn't stop to examine that bit of inane logic.

"Shall I bring the rifle?"

"No, that would give us away."

He clasped her hand and pulled her close, sliding his arm around her as he turned her away from the fire. After an awkward moment she fitted herself against him and matched her steps to his.

"Is this good?" she asked, throwing her head back and widening her smile recklessly. The motion allowed her hat to fall behind her, freeing her hair and exposing her face to the light. She was rewarded by the astonished expression on his face. Two could play games, she decided.

His smile vanished. "Yes!" he said hoarsely. "You're getting the idea. In fact—"

"Don't you dare say I'm beautiful again, Captain Colter. Even a fool would know you are only trying to frighten me." She was looking up at him, her eyes stormy, her mouth soft and inviting. "Why?"

"I'm not trying to frighten you," he answered. She couldn't know how appealing she was, or that she was tempting him to kiss her. And he couldn't resist the temptation. He curled his arm, bringing her around in front of him as he lowered his head. His lips touched hers. She froze.

"Easy," he whispered, brushing his lips back and forth against a mouth now clamped shut. She gasped, parting her lips, and he thrust his tongue inside. Her jacket fell open as he pressed against her, almost dizzy from the feel of her. He felt her arm creep around him. For a long, senseless moment he forgot what he'd started out to do. The kiss that was meant to distract Sabrina had an unexpected effect on him.

Then she pulled back, returning them to reality. Her shock was followed by fear and finally anger. She slapped him, hard, with the palm of her healing hand.

Her eyes were wide. "What was all that about?" she asked as she backed away, one hand protectively across her chest, the other behind her.

"I don't know," he admitted ruefully, "but whatever it was, it's gone."

"I see. Then I don't suppose you'll need this now, will you?" She reached down and pulled the knife from her boot.

"No. I guess I won't."

"Concealing the knife in your bedroll was what this was about, wasn't it? Don't ever try something like that again, Captain Colter, or I'll use the knife on you."

She whirled around, and moments later she was inside the blanket, eyes closed, her entire body trembling like a snow rabbit caught in the gaze of a mountain lion.

She'd known there was nothing out there, but she'd let him play out his plan, wondering how far he'd go. She hadn't expected him to kiss her. But more than that she hadn't expected the blaze of fire that the kiss had ignited, the way her body had reached out, begging to be touched, the way her lips parted, inviting him inside.

"Guess you're not going to take the first watch," he finally said.

"You guessed right, soldier." Her throat was so tight that her words came out in a breathless rush.

"Got to you, did I?" he teased, surprising himself with the lightness of his tone. "The truth is, you got to me, too. But both of us know that nothing can come of it. No two people could ever be more unsuited to each other. It won't happen again."

"You're right, Colter. It won't. As for why I responded, perhaps I have my own ways of distraction."

Her claim was brave, but he didn't believe she'd kissed him intentionally. He didn't even try to analyze the kiss. Giving thought to the combustion only fueled the flame. Best to put it behind them.

"Sweet dreams, madam jailer. I hope you don't have nightmares. I'm unarmed."

Sabrina didn't answer. He was wrong. He had a weapon, a new and powerful one against which she had no defense. He'd started a wildfire and Sabrina felt as if she were burning up.

THE WINDFLOWER

BY

SHARON AND TOM CURTIS

"Sharon and Tom's talent is immense."
—LaVyrle Spencer

With stories rich in passion and filled with humor, bestselling authors Sharon and Tom Curtis have become two of the most beloved romance novelists. Now this extraordinarily talented writing team offers a captivating tale of love and danger on the high seas, as a young woman is kidnapped and taken to an infamous privateering ship and her mysterious, golden-haired captor.

"You're very amusing, you know," he said.

For the first time since she'd left the tavern, she felt an emotion stirring within her that was not terror.

"I wasn't aware that I was being amusing," she said, a terse edge to her voice.

"I never supposed you were aware of it. But don't you think you were being a little overly conscientious? Under the circumstances."

Unfortunately his statement hit uncomfortably close to the truth. Before she could stop herself, Merry bit out, "I suppose *you* think nothing of knocking whole villages to the ground."

"Nothing at all," he said cheerfully.

"And terrorizing innocent women!" she said, a tremble in her voice.

"Yes. Innocent ones," he said, running his palm along her flat stomach, "and not so innocent ones."

She nearly fainted under his touch. "Don't do that," she said, her voice cracking in good earnest.

"Very well," he said, removing his hand. He went back to lean against the porch, resting on the heels of his hands, his long finely muscled legs stretched before him, and gave her an easy smile. "Don't run away from me, little one. For the moment you're much safer here."

Something in her face made him laugh again. "I can see you don't believe it," he continued. "But stay with me nevertheless. If you run off, I'll have to chase you, and I don't think we want to scamper across the beach like a pair of puppies."

She wondered if that meant he wouldn't invest much energy in trying to catch her if she did try to run and if it might not be worth the risk.

Reading her thoughts with alarming precision, he asked good-humoredly, "Do you think you could outrun me?"

It was hardly likely. A man used to safely negotiating the rigging during a high wind would be quick enough to catch her before she could even think of moving, and strong enough to make her very sorry. Involuntarily her gaze dropped to his hard legs, with their smooth, rhythmical blend of healthy muscle.

"Like what you see?" he asked her.

Merry's gaze flew to his, and she blushed and swallowed painfully. In a ludicrously apologetic voice she managed, "I beg your pardon."

"That's quite all right." He reached out his hand and stroked beneath her chin. "Much too conscientious. Would it surprise you to know, my little friend, that having you stare at my legs is the most uplifting thing that's happened to me all day?"

It was not the kind of remark she had remotely conceived a man might make to a woman, but there was something in his matter-of-fact delivery that made her suspect that he had participated in a great many conversations in precisely this style. Wishing she could match the ease of his tone, she said, "It's a pity your days are so dull."

"Oh, yes," he said with a glimmer of amusement, "in between knocking down villages and making people walk the plank, pirates really have very little to do."

Merry wondered briefly how she could ever have been so foolish as to have actually *wished* for an adventure.

"I don't know how you can talk about it like that," she said weakly.

He smiled. "I take it you don't usually flirt with villains."

"I don't flirt with *anyone*," Merry said, getting angry.

"I believe you don't, darling."

For a second his kind, enticing gaze studied her face, and then he looked away to the south, where a tiny flicker began to weave through the rocks. Another star of light appeared, and another, dragon's breath in the night.

"My cohorts," he observed. Offering her a hand, Devon inclined his head toward the dark-blue shadows that crept along the tavern's north side. "Come with me, I'm sure you don't want them to see you."

"*More* pirates?" said Merry hoarsely, watching the lights.

"Six more. Seven, if Reade is sober."

She hesitated, not daring to trust him, her face turned to him with the unconscious appeal of a lost child.

"Come with me," he repeated patiently. "Look at it this way. Better one dreadful pirate than seven. Whatever you're afraid I'll do to you, I can only do it once. *They* can do it seven times. Besides, I'm unarmed. You can frisk me if you want." His arm came around her back, drawing her away from the tavern. Grinning down at her, he said, "As a matter of fact, I wish you would frisk me."

She went with him, her footsteps as passive as a dreamer.

It seemed quite unnecessary to tell him. Nevertheless Merry said, "I've never met anyone like you in my life."

And don't miss these thrilling
romances from Bantam Books,
on sale in November:

ADAM'S FALL
by the *New York Times* bestselling author

Sandra Brown

Now available in paperback!

PURE SIN
by the mistress of erotic historical romance

Susan Johnson

"Susan Johnson is one of the best."
—*Romantic Times*

ON WINGS OF MAGIC
by the nationally bestselling

Kay Hooper

"[Kay Hooper] writes with exceptional beauty and
grace."
—*Romantic Times*

OFFICIAL RULES

To enter the sweepstakes below carefully follow all instructions found elsewhere in this offer.

The **Winners Classic** will award prizes with the following approximate maximum values: 1 Grand Prize: $26,500 (or $25,000 cash alternate); 1 First Prize: $3,000; 5 Second Prizes: $400 each; 35 Third Prizes: $100 each; 1,000 Fourth Prizes: $7.50 each. Total maximum retail value of Winners Classic Sweepstakes is $42,500. Some presentations of this sweepstakes may contain individual entry numbers corresponding to one or more of the aforementioned prize levels. To determine the Winners, individual entry numbers will first be compared with the winning numbers preselected by computer. For winning numbers not returned, prizes will be awarded in random drawings from among all eligible entries received. Prize choices may be offered at various levels. If a winner chooses an automobile prize, all license and registration fees, taxes, destination charges, and other expenses not offered herein are the responsibility of the winner. If a winner chooses a trip, travel must be complete within one year from the time the prize is awarded. Minors must be accompanied by an adult. Travel companion(s) must also sign release of liability. Trips are subject to space and departure availability. Certain black-out dates may apply.

The following applies to the sweepstakes named above:

No purchase necessary. You can also enter the sweepstakes by sending your name and address to: P.O. Box 508, Gibbstown, N.J. 08027. Mail each entry separately. Sweepstakes begins 6/1/93. Entries must be received by 12/30/94. Not responsible for lost, late, damaged, misdirected, illegible or postage due mail. Mechanically reproduced entries are not eligible. All entries become property of the sponsor and will not be returned.

Prize Selection/Validations: Selection of winners will be conducted no later than 5:00 PM on January 28, 1995, by an independent judging organization whose decisions are final. Random drawings will be held at 1211 Avenue of the Americas, New York, N.Y. 10036. Entrants need not be present to win. Odds of winning are determined by total number of entries received. Circulation of this sweepstakes is estimated not to exceed 200 million. All prizes are guaranteed to be awarded and delivered to winners. Winners will be notified by mail and may be required to complete an affidavit of eligibility and release of liability which must be returned within 14 days of date on notification or alternate winners will be selected in a random drawing. Any prize notification letter or any prize returned to a participating sponsor, Bantam Doubleday Dell Publishing Group, Inc., its participating divisions or subsidiaries, or the independent judging organization as undeliverable will be awarded to an alternate winner. Prizes are not transferable. No substitution for prizes except as offered or as may be necessary due to unavailability, in which case a prize of equal or greater value will be awarded. Prizes will be awarded approximately 90 days after the drawing. All taxes are the sole responsibility of the winners. Entry constitutes permission (except where prohibited by law) to use winners' names, hometowns, and likenesses for publicity purposes without further or other compensation. Prizes won by minors will be awarded in the name of parent or legal guardian.

Participation: Sweepstakes open to residents of the United States and Canada, except for the province of Quebec. Sweepstakes sponsored by Bantam Doubleday Dell Publishing Group, Inc., (BDD), 1540 Broadway, New York, NY 10036. Versions of this sweepstakes with different graphics and prize choices will be offered in conjunction with various solicitations or promotions by different subsidiaries and divisions of BDD. Where applicable, winners will have their choice of any prize offered at level-won. Employees of BDD, its divisions, subsidiaries, advertising agencies, independent judging organization, and their immediate family members are not eligible.

Canadian residents, in order to win, must first correctly answer a time limited arithmetical skill testing question. Void in Puerto Rico, Quebec and wherever prohibited or restricted by law. Subject to all federal, state, local and provincial laws and regulations. For a list of major prize winners (available after 1/29/95): send a self-addressed, stamped envelope entirely separate from your entry to: Sweepstakes Winners, P.O. Box 517, Gibbstown, NJ 08027. Requests must be received by 12/30/94. DO NOT SEND ANY OTHER CORRESPONDENCE TO THIS P.O. BOX.

Don't miss these fabulous Bantam women's fiction titles

Now on Sale

WANTED *by Patricia Potter*

Bestselling author of *Relentless*

"The healing power of love and the beauty of trust and faith in others shines like a beacon in all of Ms. Potter's work."—Romantic Times

Patricia Potter, winner of *Romantic Times*'s Storyteller of the Year Award, triumphs once more with this searing tale of an unyielding lawman and the woman caught between him and his past.

_____56600-8 *$5.50/$6.99 in Canada*

SCANDAL IN SILVER
by the highly acclaimed Sandra Chastain

"This delightful author has a tremendous talent that places her on a pinnacle reserved for special romance writers."—Affaire de Coeur

In her new *Once Upon A Time Romance,* Sandra Chastain borrows from *Seven Brides for Seven Brothers* for a wonderfully funny and sensual historical romance about five sisters stranded in the Colorado wilderness .

_____56465-X *$5.50/$6.99 in Canada*

THE WINDFLOWER
by the award-winning Sharon and Tom Curtis

"Sharon and Tom's talent is immense."—LaVyrle Spencer

This extraordinarily talented writing team offers a captivating tale — of love and danger on the high seas, about a young woman who is kidnapped and taken to an infamous privateering ship and her mysterious golden-haired captor.

_____56806-X *$4.99/$6.50 in Canada*

Don't miss these fabulous Bantam women's fiction titles

On Sale in November

ADAM'S FALL
by *New York Times* bestselling author
Sandra Brown

Blockbuster author Sandra Brown—whose name is almost synonymous with *New York Times* bestseller list—offers a classic romantic novel that aches with emotion and sizzles with passion.

❏ *56768-3 $4.99/$5.99 in Canada*

PURE SIN
by nationally bestselling **author**
Susan Johnson

From the erotic imagination of Susan Johnson comes a tale of exquisite pleasure that begins in the wilds of Montana—and ends in the untamed places of two lovers' hearts.

❏ *29956-5 $5.50/6.99 in Canada*

ON WINGS OF MAGIC
by award-winning author
Kay Hooper

Award-winning Kay Hooper offers a passionate story filled with all the humor and tenderness her fans have come to expect—a story that explores the loneliness of heartbreak and the searing power of love.

❏ *56965-1 $4.99/$5.99 in Canada*